A TRYST with EMOTIONS

A TRYST with EMOTIONS

Ten short stories

Syed Ibrahim Rizvi

GenNext Publication

ISBN: 978-93-5324-942-7

"An Imprint of Kalpaz Publication"

First Published, 2022

Published by

GenNext Publication
5, Ansari Road
Daryaganj, New Delhi-110002
Phone: 011-47034999, 9811692060
E-mail: gennextpublication@hotmail.com

Printed at: Gyan Press, Delhi.

Dedication

This book is dedicated to my father

Late Agha Rizvi

who through his genes gave me the gift

of weaving thoughts into words

Contents

Preface

Humans, as Homo sapiens, have a history of approximately 2,00,000 years on this earth. While this time span may seem to be huge when viewed in the context of our own lifespan, 2,00,000 years is just a dot in the history of life on earth.

It has taken 3.5 billion years for Darwinian evolution to create an almost infinite array of life forms. Interestingly, while all life forms differ amazingly in phenotype, there is unbelievable similarity in the biomolecules which are the building blocks of life.

Humans occupy a unique position in the evolutionary tree. The development of brain and the advent of cognitive powers have made Sapiens masters of the planet earth. Among all living creatures, Homo sapiens are the only creatures which have the power to create fictional thoughts.

The ability to delve into fiction has created the art of weaving thoughts into words. The documentation of fictional thought process, through words, results into stories which the human mind can visualise without actually experiencing the event.

This compilation of ten short stories is a result of the wandering of the human brain seeking to piece together the nuances of varied human emotions.

The present compilation of short stories explores romantic love, teenage crush, destiny, patriotism, tragedy and drama. The book would make an interesting companion for an audience with an interest in English language.

Syed Ibrahim Rizvi

Acknowledgement

My first book '*A Kaleidoscope of Thoughts*' published in 2020 was very well received by the audience. A huge number of well wishers congratulated and encouraged me to continue my journey into literature. I acknowledge all my peers who have been eloquent in their praise for my short stories. I would be failing in my duty if I do not acknowledge the dedicated teachers of my first school, the Boys High School, Allahabad, who took pains to instil in me the subtlety of English language.

Syed Ibrahim Rizvi

1

I couldn't say 'I love you'

She was not a classical beauty. A heavy eyebrow accentuated the eyes. Thick black hair made the forehead look small. At first sight she personified a typical Indian middle-class girl. As she approached the Biochemistry department on that forenoon of July, taking care to lift her trousers a little bit protecting her steps from the puddles of water on the road, she walked briskly shielding her face from the soft drizzle. While she climbed the two stairs at the entrance of the department building, she certainly didn't notice the gawky boy in brown corduroy pants and white shirt. However, I did find her beautiful.

This was the first day after the summer vacations and I was now a student of the final year M Sc. That day sitting in the classroom with friends, my thoughts wandered several times to the lingering image of the girl whom I had seen that morning. Later in the afternoon I again saw her as part of a group talking in hushed tones standing before the office of the Head of the Department. I came to understand that this was the new batch of first year undergraduate students and today was their first day in the department.

A few weeks passed, I would try to go to the Department early and stand on the stairs keeping an eye on that beautiful girl while she walked towards the department, took the two stairs and passed without a glance. It became a routine and I became addicted to this daily exercise. After a few days I realised that while I stood on the stairs each day my heart beats became a bit louder. A strange sensation engulfed me while she approached and walked past me.

Henceforth life became a bit different for me. She started coming into my thoughts even while I went back home. Cricket matches on the television now didn't excite me. It was more pleasurable to think about her while I lay lazily on the bed. I started giving more thought to lyrics of romantic songs rather than humming the tune. My mind continuously played the everyday episode of her walking past me. I started dreaming about her.

Although the classes of first year undergraduate took place on the first floor, I could catch a glimpse of her several times in a day. Each glimpse now became a moment of joy for me. I found out her name. She was Neelu. Now my thoughts had a name to dream.

Something happened perceptibly but very slowly after a few weeks. I realised that while she walked towards the department, she was a bit conscious of her looks. The carefree approach was gone and her strides became measured. Her eyes were always on the floor and she walked in a hurry. I could not make out what this new turn of events signalled. A few weeks down the line, I figured out that she would gaze at me when I was not looking towards her, however her eyes would move away as soon as I looked at her.

After a couple of months, I confided my state of mind to a couple of my female batch mates. They counselled me to shrug off my shyness and talk to Neelu. Easier said than done, I could not muster the courage of walking up to her. Even if I walked to her, I did not understand what I must say. Every day my two friends would push me to talk to Neelu but all my valour would dissipate.

I now knew without a doubt that Neelu had full idea about my feelings for her. She would pass me in the corridor with a smile. She probably had an inkling that my two friends also knew about my feelings and were sometimes coaxing me to muster the courage of talking to her. It is now after forty years that I realise how difficult it was in the 1980's to talk to a girl, far less to express feeling of love to her.

Two years passed in a flurry. I would see her, my eyes would follow her, she would gaze at me but be shy of meeting the gaze. I would wait for her at the entrance, she would now walk slowly. I would follow her behind her rikshaw when she went home and she would also give me a glance ensuring that I got the message.

The final exams heralded the end of the course. I never realised that the joy of completing the M Sc course would be accompanied with the sadness of losing Neelu. I did not see her again in the University. The first few weeks were difficult, she continued to come in my dreams but the harsh reality of choosing an academic career engulfed my mind and I became engrossed in research.

Time began to fly. The long years of research leading to Ph D were both exciting and difficult. The joy of research, the feeling of achievement after a research paper, the conferences, and the chance of going abroad were more than a handful for the mind to think about Neelu. She did creep into thoughts once a while but fleetingly.

Fortunately, I got appointment just after completing Ph D and then got a chance to go abroad for post doc. It was just after I returned that my mother one day brought up the topic of marriage. She asked me whether I had someone in mind and expectedly, to her satisfaction, I said I had no girl in mind. Customarily, she did ask me about my preferences and again expectedly, and to her satisfaction, I did not say a word. I now realise I was never smart enough in matters concerning mate selection. Else I would have at least spoken my mind to Neelu.

Marriage was a typical middle class arranged affair. I saw the face of my wife only after wedding! This is something which makes the arranged marriages so durable. All the action starts after the marriage. My wife Uzma was a simple girl with typical Indian values. I enjoyed the after-marriage scene with great pleasure. Everything was new and there was so much to discover. The long hours when we talked was more or less focussed on my Ph. D. days, experiences abroad and hobbies. Uzma listened intuitively to all my banter. It was in one of my candid moods that I told her about Neelu.

My story probably had so much emotion that she expressed empathy with me. Neelu was now just a story.

We were married in November and the first year was a dream sequence. The first drops of rain in the month of July provided the perfect setting for cupid to exert its influence. Uzma looked prettier than ever. That afternoon, in the green ensemble she looked stunning. Overcast sky and the drizzle made a perfect romantic setting. As I returned from University, she asked me whether I would be willing to go to Civil Lines.

We had stopped at a famous footwear shop in Civil Lines, Uzma was window shopping and I was biding time in the corridor. Amidst the soft drizzle, there were few people on the street. My gaze wandered in forward direction and I stopped for a moment. At the end of the corridor, stood Neelu. She was wearing a maroon dress which made her look gorgeous. She was looking towards me. My trance was broken when Uzma prodded me that she was done with the shopping. I found it difficult to shake my gaze off Neelu. After a few moments, I spoke to Uzma and asked her whether she remembers the story I had told her about the girl who was my crush during M Sc days.

Uzma asked me to go and talk to Neelu. I felt the same feeling when I was coaxed by my friends but could not find the courage. In reply I came up with a weird request. I asked Uzma to go to Neelu and ask the obvious question, whether she was the same Neelu? Uzma didn't take a moment and to my surprise walked towards Neelu.

She spoke a few words which I didn't listen and then from the distance waived me to come to them.

This walk of thirty yards was perhaps the most exciting of my life's moments. I gingerly walked thinking frantically what I was expected to say to Neelu, a bygone crush, in the company of my beloved wife. I reached the place where Neelu and Uzma were standing and as I was about to say something, my voice was drowned by the horn of a vehicle just a few meters away. A car had stopped just beside the corridor. Neelu looked towards the car and immediately walked towards it. The man on the wheels opened the door next to him and Neelu slid into the companion seat. The car moved on.

Fortunately Uzma did not understand my feelings. She took my arm and told that she was feeling hungry. I looked towards the direction of the car and realised that I had lost Neelu once again. Would life give another chance to say: I love you.

2

Our eyes met and she froze

The bus conductor announced that our destination had arrived. The town of Mohammadabad Gohna, near Azamgarh, was too small to have a proper bus stop. A couple of roadside tea stalls under the shade of a neem tree was the only landmark for the bus stop. Weary from the six-hour bus ride in summer heat we slowly got down from the bus counting our bags and taking care of the earthen pot which was the water storing option. A few rickshaws with slanting seats beckoned the passengers. Walidpur, our final destination, was still a couple of kilometres away. We were about to reach our maternal grandparent's home for spending the next two months far from the sweltering heat of the city.

As the rickshaw made its way through the narrow mud splintered paths, I could sense that nothing had changed since last year. Time seems to take its own time in these villages. Every soul looked contended, no tension and no worry were visible on smiling faces. Even the pace of walk was slow compared to the always-on-the-run attitude of my city.

The scene at grandparent's house was no different. One year had passed since my visit last summer but nothing looked different. Afternoons seemed so long. There was a perceptible evening time when kids of similar age from the locality assembled to play the country games be it *kabaddi, kho kho* or *gulli danda*. I found no difficulty in melting into the village lifestyle.

The next day somebody brought a rubber ball and we decided to play *chibbhi-phod*. The game involves two teams each taking turn to dislodge the pyramid of clay pieces by throwing the ball. If dislodged, the team had to again assemble the pyramid while the other team try their best to hit an opposite member with the ball.

We had divided the eight individuals into two teams. Except for my younger brother who was seven years old and a good five years younger to me, I didn't know any of the other members of the two teams. Despite the unfamiliarity, there was no dearth of camaraderie. Leading the opposite team was a petite girl by the name of Ghazala. She was a livewire with a face which had an overdose of smile. She must have been ten or eleven.

The game continued for almost an hour with both teams doing their best to hit and reconstruct the *chibbhi*. Abruptly someone called out Ghazala from the other side of the boundary wall and she ran off without even completing her team's turn to throw the ball.

After a few days, the late afternoon games became routine. I came to understand that Ghazala was also visiting her grandparents for the summer vacations. Once she told me that she was in class eight. The other kids were from the village itself and studied in the madrasa which was on the other side of the village lake.

The days gave way to weeks and the two months passed within no time. My father had come to take us back to Allahabad. We started early morning from Walidpur crossing the pontoon bridge over the river Tons, found the bus from Mohammadabad Gohna and reached Allahabad in the evening.

This was the year when I was to take the Class X board exams. Life in Allahabad was so different. We were mad about cricket. TV was a new addition to our home and it was extremely difficult to coerce oneself into studies. Exams came and went. I got 67% marks which was a great moment of joy for my parents. At that time getting a first division was important, percentage did not matter.

Summer vacations came and again we were outbound to Walidpur to our grandparent's home. I found my fishing rod exactly at the same place where I had tucked it last year. The village bazaar oozed the same aroma, and the river Tons flowed as if one year interval was just a dot in its history. In the afternoon I met the same friends. Everybody had grown in the last twelve months. Junaid sported a visible beard and a white skull cap. My eyes wandered aimlessly as if something was missing. It was late in the afternoon that Ghazala appeared. She had changed a lot from last year. The most noticeable difference was the headscarf that she wore.

The afternoon games were played with the same intensity; however, I could sense a change in the attitude of Ghazala. Now she was a little circumspect of coming close to any of the boys. One day in the midst of a game she had the ball in hand and it was me who she had to throw at. At this time, I looked into her eyes. For a moment she froze. The look on her face said something which was difficult to understand. I also felt a dash of adrenaline. All this happened in a flash. She hit me with the ball and the game continued.

Time passed and days became weeks. The afternoon games became a moment of anticipation for me. Somehow, I would find pleasure in all that Ghazala did. She was running for the ball and suddenly she slipped. She was in pain and I was the one nearest to her. I knelt beside her and touched her ankle and she looked towards me. The loud thud of her falling was heard inside the house also. My mother came running and saw me sitting beside Ghazala. She helped Ghazala on her feet and guided her to the narrow path to her house in the neighbourhood.

The next day, everybody came for the afternoon game except Ghazala. I played but my mind was not in the game. I recollected how she had looked at me when I had touched her ankle. The moment had been frozen in my mind and I played it again and again. My summer vacations were almost finished and, in a few days, father came to take us back to Allahabad.

This year when we returned to Allahabad, among the routine village items which included jaggery, vinegar, and mango pickles, I carried with me the sweet memory of Ghazala. It was after my return that I realised that the thoughts of Ghazala brought a certain kind of pleasure which was felt not in the brain but in the heart. This feeling I had not encountered before. Ghazala had become a constant companion in my thoughts.

The year was indeed very long. Months passed slowly. Days were long and nights full of dreams. Memories of Ghazala continued to haunt me. I longed for the summer vacations and our trip to Walidpur. It was the mid of April, the day when I returned from college, I found my mother in a sullen mood. She told that letter had come from Walidpur informing that grandmother was very ill and that we will have to visit Walidpur in a few days.

This trip to Walidpur was so different. The mood in the house was of sadness. Grandmother was in diabetic coma and the village had no hospital. That night she passed away peacefully in sleep. After a few days we returned to Allahabad.

The whole perception of summer vacation changed. Walidpur now had a different meaning. Grandfather was alone and everyone was concerned to find a solution. It was decided that grandfather would leave the ancestral house and move to Allahabad with us. This decision was in effect the end of Walidpur for me. Deep in my heart I wanted to have a glimpse of Ghazala. Did she come to Walidpur for summer vacations this year? I had no way to find an answer. Life moved on.

The University days were fun. The experience of co-education brought new excitement into life. I realised that girls in the college were much more forthcoming in their attitude compared to my cultural upbringing. Going out for fun or to a movie was no big deal. I also realised that relationships were ephemeral. It was in these complex human associations that moral values took a back seat. In the din of glitz and glamour accentuated with fake beauty, I sometimes missed the rustic innocence of Ghazala.

Time flew. My life was preoccupied with books, studies and college. Free time meant reading Frederick Forsyth, Sidney Sheldon and Leon Uris. The time spent abroad for higher studies was also capsulated in defined roles. The joy of science preoccupied my mind and I became a loner with few friends. Returning to India was never difficult and fortunately found a teaching job very soon.

I had seen thirty summers when one afternoon I was confronted with the idea of marriage with mother informing that she had a very good girl in mind who was doing masters in Aligarh. I did not say anything. It is an interesting situation that in our culture, no answer is presumed to be a passive 'yes'. That night when I lay in bed, I realised that I had reached the point in life where I must fulfil the Darwin's purpose of life. I was expected to find a mate for generations to continue.

Before I slept, my mind wandered to the time spent with numerous girls at different phases in life. I also remembered Neelu, my muse during two years of college, to whom I could never talk. With these romantic thoughts I dozed off that night. *Her face was tantalizingly close, our eyes were locked. Her sinless face was beaming with an innocent smile and the open lips wanted to say something.*

Ghazala came into my dream. I woke up at 2 am, I realised I was perspiring.

The marriage had been fixed. Uzma, my prospective life partner, had completed her MSc from Aligarh University. Indian marriages are more inclined towards the joys and pleasures of relatives than the likes/dislikes of bride and groom. So was mine. Finally, the *barat* returned from Aligarh and Uzma was my bride destined to be with me for the rest of my life. From now onwards it was a sin to even think of Neelu or numerous girlfriends. Ghazala should also be a part of history.

The room was heavily decorated. The bed had a canopy of flowers. Uzma was in bright red traditional clothes with an assortment of jewellery. Her drape, heavily embroidered, covered her face. My mother had silently pushed in my hands a box while I was entering the bridal room. I cautiously opened the box and found a ring and an anklet. Some sixth sense told me that these were intended to be my first gift to my wife.

Gingerly I took Uzma's left hand in my hands and placed the ring on her ring finger. Then I took out the anklet and slightly put my hands on her feet exposing her ankle. With both hands I tried to put the anklet in place. I experienced a strange sensation; the touch of her ankle caused an adrenaline rush. I froze. Ghazala overtook my senses. *Ghazala was on the ground clutching her ankle and I was conforting her.* For a moment I forgot that I was sitting beside Uzma. The unexpected turn of events made Uzma apprehensive, she removed her face covering drape and looked directly at me. Our eyes met; we both froze in sight. This moment had no end. In that bright red bridal suit, sitting amorously before me, was indeed Ghazala.

Twenty years had passed since our last visit to Walidpur. My grandparent's house was in bad shape. The hand pump stood its place although the handle had broken off. The courtyard was empty. Ghazala picked a few pieces of mud pebbles from the ground and placed them one top of another. She was recreating the *chibbhi-phod* game which made us come together.

3

The Last Wish

The *muezzin* called the *azan* inviting the faithful to the mosque. This ritual has been going on everyday in the small mosque situated at the end of the narrow lane. The lane had a blind end finishing off in front of the dilapidated house which was home to five families. Seven decades back, Khaliq had moved into this house with his family of five sons and two daughters. Khaliq owned a tonga and earned a decent living. Time passed and it became difficult to maintain the horse. Cheaper modes of transport made tonga an unviable alternative, the wheels of tonga finally stopped. Khaliq passed away in 1965.

The house was now inherited by the five sons, two of them who were already married. The five equal divisions resulted in construction of walls which demarcated single rooms for each family. Ahmad the eldest son worked as a rickshaw mechanic, toiling hard he somehow managed to feed his family of three sons and three daughters. As time passed, the single room inherited space became too small for the growing family and Ahmad moved out of the room into the outside lane finding a space just sufficient for a small cot in front of the mosque. The lane in front of the mosque now became even narrower.

Poverty comes with several additional burdens. After the marriage of the three daughters, Ahmad and wife Sakina felt an immediate void in their life. The three sons were too hard pressed with their own travails to take care of their old parents. The new technology had given rise to battery operated rickshaw and suddenly the cycle rickshaw become history. In the backdrop of new technology, Ahmad lost his means of earning.

The narrow lane now became Ahmad and Sakina's permanent living place. Thanks to protruding balcony of the adjoining houses, the cot had partial protection from rain. The faithful coming to the mosque provided the only means of earning to Ahmad. Strange are the manifestations of faith among the faithful. It gives satisfaction to the faithful to give alms to people who throng the places of worship. Ahmad and Sakina became regular beneficiary for many of the faithful who came to the mosque.

Paradoxically while time seems to fly for the affluent, it crawls for the poor. Ahmad's life was so mired in hardships that regular problems hardly affected his life. In today's materialistic world while many vouch and practice intermittent fasting to keep fit, Ahmad and Sakina had long made eating once a day their normal practice.

Seasons came and went however nothing changed for Ahmad. Suddenly something happened which made life even worse for the couple. Somebody told that a new disease was affecting people and that the government had imposed lockdown for three weeks. Disease and death now evoked no fear for Ahmad and Sakina, for them life had become a ritual which was a burden to be endured.

The *muezzin* called the *azan*. Today a few policemen had visited the mosque and pasted a notice that the mosque cannot hold a prayer for more than five people. For fear of police not even five people turned up at the mosque that morning. While the faithful stayed away, Ahmad and Sakina lost their only livelihood. After a few days they had almost nothing to eat. Survival henceforth depended on the generosity of the neighbourhood.

With the imposition of the lockdown, constant hunger became a new normal. While Sakina could visit a few adjoining houses and was fortunate to get some food, Ahmad was too weak to get up. His ulcer was now giving him sleepless nights. The pain was becoming almost unbearable. His face had become a constant grimace which camouflaged the continuous pain. It was after a week into lockdown that Ahmad breathed his last while gazing at the sky lying on the five feet cot at the door of the mosque.

Despite the loss of moral values in the present times, death is still an event which unites. The neighbourhood opened its heart and provided Sakina with food and money for the next few days. Poverty is a phenomenon which changes the definition of most human emotions. Losing life partner meant availability of more space for

Sakina to position her cot at the front of the mosque's entrance. Life moved on.

Rumours started doing rounds that a new law had been enacted which made mandatory for all citizens to carry an identity card. Those not possessing an identity card would be arrested and put into detention centres. The neighbourhood was abuzz with activity. People were digging into their long lost documents to find proof of their domicile. The area corporator had opened his office and was charging Rs 500 for assisting identity card aspirants.

Sakina also heard the news of the impending new law and the possibility of being deported to detention centre. After the death of Ahmad she had been able to save Rs 500 from the money which people had given her to tide over the crisis. It was a sunny day and Sakina walked to the nearest market. She found the shop that sold small tin boxes. She bought one painted tin box with a provision for lock on the latch.

The underneath of the cot was the only place where Sakina could keep her belongings and she placed the locked box under the cot. That afternoon she slept peacefully.

The old and the young, healthy and infirm, and the rich and the poor, everyone made efforts to get the identity card. Old land records, long forgotten school certificates, voter slips, and sundry receipts, all contributed to affirming the requirements of the identity card. Despite being advised, coaxed and encouraged, Sakina did not go to the municipal corporation office for filling the application for the identity card.

Information was rife that police had raided the adjoining locality and checked the identity cards of the residents. A few who could not produce the required document were arrested and taken away. There was a strong possibility of the raid being conducted near the mosque the next day. Sakina woke up early that Friday morning. She checked the tin box under the cot. The box and the lock were intact. A faint smile crossed her face. She looked contended.

That day Sakina took a bath using the common municipal facility. Taking bath had long become a luxury. She dressed herself in the green cotton suit, the dress which someone had given her this Eid perhaps fulfilling the requirement of the mandatory Zakat. It had been almost two months since she had kempt her hairs. Today she bought a sachet of hair oil and applied it to her silver hair. From under the pillow she took out a broken mirror and looked at herself.

Mirrors never lie. However, today the mirror which was reflecting the face of Sakina had a different story to tell. Sakina found herself looking at a girl of seventeen years in a loud makeup with exciting dreams writ large on the beaming face. She was the bride looking at herself just before the nikah was to be solemnized. Sakina's memory wandered to the next milestone of life when Jawed, her first son, was born. The *muezzin* started the *azan* and the blaring of the out of tune loudspeaker jolted Sakina. She realised that in the mirror she was looking at a wrinkled face which had several tragic stories within its fold.

Sakina waited for the police party to arrive and check the identity cards. The day passed but nothing happened. She overheard that due to a law-and-order problem the raids did not happen today. Most probably the police party would make a checking drive near the mosque tomorrow. For someone whose life was but a daily routine of day and night, one day did not make any difference.

A couple of days back someone had died in the locality. There was some sort of a religious ceremony after the Friday prayers. Sakina too had received an invitation. The biryani was served after the religious discourse. The host wanted to feed the poor in the hope to bless the departed. Sakina took two helpings of the biryani. She had not eaten such a stomach full for months. She felt nice and happy.

Thinking of tomorrow Sakina curled herself on the five feet cot that evening. It was a rare occasion when she was not battling hunger pangs. Today she was contended. Due to power breakdown, night descended early in the locality. Even at 8 pm, the lane was empty. Most families had partaken the meal served as part of religious ceremony for the dead, and hence there were no cries of children finding it hard to sleep on an empty stomach.

Sakina slept peacefully that night. She did not know the time but suddenly she woke up with a lump in her stomach. There was a feeling of nausea which gripped her. She thought it was a result of binge eating the previous afternoon. She again dozed off.

Sakina felt another bout of nausea. She again felt a lump somewhere up in the chest. She wanted to cry but could not find her voice. Her hands felt unduly heavy. Her mind wandered. *She was sitting with Ahmad in an alien land. The grass was green and the trees were tall. At a distance there was a wired boundary, but it was far away. She was eating lunch served by some unknown people. She was happy and contended.*

Sakina felt an unknown sensation. She was choking. Her body was getting limp. She tried to understand what was happening. *She was finding bliss, she was like a sparrow flying from the cot to the minaret of the mosque. There was a mirage. A huge kaleidoscope of lights engulfed her. She was wafting in the sky.*

The *muezzin* was calling the morning *azan*. The sun was still some distance below the horizon. The few faithful who arrived for the prayers and walked past the cot in front of the mosque entrance were oblivious of the fact that Sakina was no more. Her face did not reflect the pain of death which she had experienced a couple of hours back.

The morning brought life back in the lane. Half naked children started playing. Someone carried tea in the plastic bag. The vegetable vendor was selling his merchandise. It was late in the morning that somebody noticed that flies had begun to gather on the face of Sakina. News spread fast. Again, the death in the locality made everyone come together. The space for a cot had fallen vacant in front of the mosque.

Sakina's elder son found the key tied to her mother's head scarf. The tin box was opened. Packed neatly inside were two sets of clothes, a bathing soap and a washing bar for the clothes. Beneath the clothes, safely put in a plastic cover, was a black and white wedding photograph of a seventeen-year-old bride with a young Ahmad.

Unfortunately, Sakina could not realise her dream of being deported into a detention centre. At least, in detention, she would not have to worry for the next meal.

4

For a few extra yards

August, 2009

The cavalcade consisted of five vehicles. Decked with flowers, the motorcade moved slowly towards Islampur, a tiny hamlet in the eastern Uttar Pradesh town of Ghazipur. Subedar Jameel looked calm. Despite his heavily plastered right leg, he was standing on the open jeep. The fleet of vehicles reached the hamlet's most revered spot, the pedestal on which the bust of Brigadier Suleman was mounted. Subedar Jameel went down the open jeep and placed a garland on the bust of his illustrious grandfather. This was indeed a proud moment, the victor of Pakistani outpost number 5 was paying homage to the lion of Mahshera, one who had destroyed Pakistani army's most important outpost in the 1948 war. As Jameel stood before the bust, dreary eyed, his thoughts wandered to the memories of that fateful day when he had captured the enemy post killing ten Pakistani soldiers, one of them being the descendent of this great soul on whose head he had just placed the garland.

October 1948

There was a strange heaviness in the air. Islampur had never witnessed such a divide. Bashiruddin had been teaching in the local secondary school for the last thirty-two years. Today when he entered the class, he observed that the students were sitting in two separate groups. The communal divide was more than visible. Returning home that afternoon Bashiruddin felt a deep sense of helplessness. Is this the price of Independence from the British? Local newspapers were full of vitriolic messages exhorting the members of the minority community to migrate to Pakistan.

The local community leaders were also active in fanning communal hatred. Although Islampur was still not affected by violence but reports from other parts of India were very disturbing. Bashiruddin just could not understand the logic of partition of the country on the basis of religion. In his thirty-two years of teaching, he had preached that religion was a tool to follow a righteous path. How could religion suddenly become an instrument to divide the nation?

Among his three sons, Bashiruddin had an inkling that Suleman, the eldest, was the brightest. The youngest Zamir was the most difficult. Bashiruddin had an idea that Zamir was frequently visiting local religious leaders and harboured some radical feelings.

The atmosphere of Islampur worsened. Several Muslim families had left the village heading for Pakistan. People had become wary of venturing out alone in mixed neighbourhoods. Bashiruddin felt heavy at heart. On that day when the family sat for dinner, it was around halfway that Zamir broke the silence. Without meeting the eyes, he said loudly that he intended to go to Pakistan tomorrow with a family which lived a few houses away. Bashiruddin felt a lump in his throat. He could never imagine that someone from his family would be so unpatriotic so as to leave the homeland. The look on the face of Zamir was nonchalant. Everybody knew it was worthless to argue.

Life moved on, Bashiruddin breathed his last a few years after partition, however in Suleman he had left his legacy. Suleman was bright in every aspect and wanted to uphold his father's patriotic instincts. He qualified the National Defence Academy examination and became a proud officer in the Indian army. Brigadier Suleman became a legend and died fighting the Pakistani army.

April 2009

The word haveli was a misnomer. What remained of the ancestral house were only a few rooms with leaking roofs and walls which resembled rubble. Jameel had received news that he had been selected for the Indian army as a non-commissioned officer. The worn-out outer door of the house proudly displayed the nameplate: Subedar Jameel.

Fifty years is a long time. Islampur had forgotten the pangs of partition and was back to its roots. The age-old traditions have been revived. The temple's kirtan would pause while the *muezzin* recited the *azan* in the adjoining mosque. Every Thursday, there was a trickle of village women to the bust of Brigadier Suleman where they placed sacred flowers in obeisance to the martyr.

The television set in Jameel's room broke the news. War had become inevitable. The enemy had intruded several sectors across the border. That evening, through a messenger, Subedar Jameel received information from the army high command to report immediately to the base camp at Jammu. Before proceeding to join his command, Jameel went to his grandfather's memorial where he recited the *fateha* and silently prayed.

Helicopters ferried the army unit of Subedar Jameel to the forward post. The temperature was below freezing. The eerie silence of the hills told a story which was far removed from the romance which poets usually weave in their songs. The platoon had been extensively briefed by the commanding officer. The task was cut out. Indian territory had to reclaimed and also the strategic forward post code number 5 of the enemy was to be captured.

The last camp of the platoon commandeered by Subedar Jameel was between a cliff and a gorge. The attack was to start at 4 am. Nobody slept. A makeshift temple and a mosque was setup at the camp. Although the places of worship were different, significantly the faithful showed no discrimination between both the places of worship.

The attack was underway, the first shot was fired just before dawn. The enemy was taken by surprise but the retaliation was swift. A heavy barrage of fire was being exchanged. The terrain was difficult and only a small distance separated the opposite armies. Subedar Jameel was leading from the front. His rifle vision caught a glimpse of a movement and the burst from the gun brought down a body rolling down the ridge.

The battle for forward post 5 went on for four long hours. The intensity of the gunfire slowly decreased from both sides. Jameel was inching close to enemy camp, he could sense the forward post of enemy barely a few meters away. The bodies of enemy soldiers lay strewn. Jameel had also lost nine of his soldiers. Grenade shrapnels had injured Jameel however he kept moving forward, his hand proudly held the tricolour.

He had received two bullets in the stomach. Barely able to move, the Pakistani soldier was waiting to die. His ammunition had finished. He checked his emergency revolver, there was only one bullet left. The pain was unbearable, he wished to die. His mind wandered, Zehra was waiting for him at his ancestral house in *Buzurga* village of Sialkot. They had been married just six months back. Before he received the duty call, Zehra had told him that she was pregnant. He carried the photo of Zehra in his inside pocket but he did not have the strength to pull it out.

The pain was becoming intense. Death was inevitable. The soldier took the revolver in his hand and pointed to his head, perhaps the last bullet would end his agony. Suddenly he heard a sound. An Indian soldier with a flag was slowly crawling towards his side. The soldier pointed the revolver towards the enemy and was about to pull the trigger. His mind again wandered to the image of expectant Zehra. He realised that the other soldier with the flag was like him. He too was fighting a war for invisible stakes. Probably a 'Zehra' would be waiting for this Indian soldier somewhere in his country. Almost two dozen soldiers have lost their lives for a few extra yards of barren land.

Jameel went past the Pakistani soldier thinking him to be dead. He reached the place where the green flag of Pakistan was still fluttering. Subedar Jameel snatched the green and white flag from the post and mounted the tricolour. The sun was shining bright. Forward post number 5 had been captured.

A faint voice interrupted Jameel. He heard someone say 'brother, can you give me some water'. The Pakistani soldier was in intense pain. Sometimes even death plays tricks, it makes you wait. Jameel understood the agony of the dying soldier. A pint of water still remained in his water bottle. Jameel opened the bottle and poured some into the parched open mouth of the Pakistani soldier.

His mind again took him to Sialkot. It was spring time and there were kites in the sky. A kite had cut another kite in the sky. He could barely make out the face of the Indian soldier who had just put some water in his mouth. Angels are even found on the battlefield.

The water made the Pakistani soldier speak to his Indian counterpart. He had grown up in Sialkot watching Indian movies. The soldier told Jameel that he too had an Indian connection; his grandfather had migrated to Pakistan in 1948. Grandfather had told him that they belonged to a small village named Islampur in Ghazipur district of Uttar Pradesh.

The Pakistani soldier tried to smile. Perhaps death was waiting for this moment. His face became silent and his breathing stopped. Jameel covered the face of the Pakistani soldier with his towel which was already soaked with his blood. For some moments he sat beside the dead man, a silent prayer went through his lips. He recited the *fateha* for the departed kin.

5

Love in the autumn zone

The aging lines on the face were not heavy enough to prevent Raj from recognizing Rashmi, who stood amidst the waiting crowd at the gate of the St Joseph's college, on that cold January afternoon. It was almost noon and the guardians were waiting for the gate to open to pick their wards from the college. Raj had been coming daily for this chore, dropping and picking his grandson, and had developed a routine of sorts. The crowd at the gate was more or less the same everyday. Except a few glances and a short wave of the hand, no one seemed interested in striking a conversation.

Things had not gone well for Rashmi this morning. She had to wake up in the wee hours because her daughter became suddenly unwell. There was a crisis of sorts at home because there was no one to take Anand, her grandson, to school. Her daughter suggested that she accompany Anand to the St Joseph's college and also bring him back.

Rashmi waited for the college gate to open standing at the far corner of the waiting area space. She found the crowd immersed in their mobile phones. It was almost unexpectedly that her moving gaze caught the sight of the man in blue shirt with a countenance that was on the other side of sixty, standing in the far corner. Somewhere in the recess of her brain she could recollect having known this person. Her mind went into overdrive trying to recollect her memory. It was on the third gaze that she recognised Raj who was her batchmate almost half a century back while she was a student of undergraduate at Allahabad University.

Rashmi's thought catapulted her to that January morning, about fifty years back, when she had entered the Allahabad University Science Faculty for attending her first B Sc class in the Botany department. She had stepped into the University for the first time and the thought of coeducation was both exciting and strange. She found that the girls were huddled in a discreet bunch. She gingerly joined the group of girls not by any preconceived thought but by pure instinct.

Thoughts came tumbling forth in that moment of waiting for Rashmi. She vividly recollected how, almost as an unsaid rule, the girls would sit in the front benches and the boys would take the back benches. Rashmi's mind also played back the moment when a boy coming late had sneaked on to the second bench where she was sitting and she had instantly put her bag between herself and the boy. Rashmi recollected the sight of that boy and the sheepish grin thereafter. She realised that despite the age, Raj had not lost the sparkle in his eyes.

Rashmi's ongoing thought was suddenly punctuated by the ringing of the school bell and the creaking of the college gate. She looked towards the point where Raj was standing. Raj had already gone inside the school. Rashmi found Anand, her grandson, in front of his class and walked to her car.

That evening Raj felt more energetic. While he walked his daily evening stroll, he did not feel pain in his knees. His mind took him to the moment when he was a student of B Sc at Allahabad University. He remembered Rashmi, the beautiful girl who was so well behaved. A smile crossed his lips when his mind reminded him the moments when he had reached the Botany class late and sat on the second bench where Rashmi was sitting. He still remembered the brown bag that suddenly found its way between him and Rashmi.

Rashmi's daughter was still unwell and this necessitated that Rashmi would again take Anand to school. An unknown emotion made Rashmi look forward to the task at hand. The scene at the St Joseph gate was without any change. Rashmi's eyes wandered, without any overt reason, looking to spot Raj. She found Raj in his same corner. He was gazing towards Rashmi, trying to fathom the events that might have happened in her life in these fifty years. Their eyes met each other's gaze. Both felt uncertain how to react. It was on the second eye contact that Raj could sense some affirmation from Rashmi. He smiled, she nodded. He started walking towards her. The school bell rang.

Returning home that afternoon, Rashmi's thoughts kept on drifting to the fleeting moment when she met

Raj. Fifty years is a long time to remember anyone. She realised that while in University she had never talked to Raj. Her strict upbringing at home kept her out of bounds to most members of the opposite sex.

Raj found it hard not to think about Rashmi. He realised that there was a surge of adrenaline when he had walked towards Rashmi this afternoon and exchanged a few words. The school bell had rung before giving him more time beyond the pleasantries. Looking at Rashmi, his eyes had taken him back in time. He found that he was looking at a beautiful eighteen-year-old girl with a bag slung over the shoulder. As if on impulse, Raj realised that he was already looking forward to the chore of going to the college the next day.

In a few days, the small daily interlude at the gate of St Joseph's college became the most pleasant moment of the day for both Raj and Rashmi. Raj could find out that Rashmi had a troubled marriage and that she was now separated. Beyond this information Rashmi had never divulged more details. Raj was more forthcoming in his life story. He confided that his wife had passed away a couple of years back and that he lived with his son.

It was the third week of February. The routine of standing together at the gate with intermittent conversation had become a regular feature in Raj and Rashmi's daily life. That day, just before the scheduled time of school giving over, there was an announcement that due to some sports related activity the school will give over one hour later.

While some guardians opted to stay put at the gate, others dispersed to attend to their routines. Raj suggested to Rashmi that they walk to the Alfred Park just on the other side of the road. An awkward moment later, both Raj and Rashmi crossed the road on way to the park. They found an empty bench in the shade. Raj suggested that they sit down for some time. Rashmi felt uncomfortable, her eyes involuntarily scanned the presence of other people in her peripheral vision. The guilt of sharing a bench with Raj reminded her of the day when Raj had found a seat next to her in the Botany class and she had put her bag to keep a distance. Despite the guilt, an unknown instinct made her happy. There was a feeling of content which she had not experienced for a long time.

On the way back to school, the traffic on the road had increased with guardians vying for vacant spaces to park their vehicles. A scooterist lost balance and Rashmi had to take an evasive action. She tripped. On an impulse Raj caught her arm and steadied her. In that moment of tripping, Raj caught a glimpse of Rashmi's wide-open eyes. Rashmi felt a rush of adrenaline. She momentarily blushed.

The school gave over and it was routine again. That afternoon, Rashmi's thought reminded her again and again of the moments she spent with Raj. She was getting utterly confused. Why did she walk with Raj to the park? What would happen if anyone had recognised her? Despite the pressing questions which her mind threw at her, Rashmi felt an uneasy joy. Today she felt hungry and looked forward to dinner.

Raj also replayed the events of this afternoon. He realised that he felt much younger and healthy in the company of Rashmi. The garlanded picture of his late wife Sunita stared at him from the wall in the room. Raj felt confused. His mind took him to the moment when in an impulsive gesture he had held Rashmi's hand preventing her from tripping. His mind could not answer why that gesture gave him a feeling of happiness?

It was Holi time. The school was going to close for a week for festival holidays. It had become almost a practice that Raj would come about ten minutes before and take the spot where he would be joined by Rashmi in a few minutes. In the last few months, their conversation had slowly veered from pleasantries to mundane. Rashmi now felt a lot more comfortable in the company of Raj. This afternoon, on the eve of Holi, Rashmi found Raj with a glint of mischief in his eyes. As Rashmi looked towards the other side, a hand brushed her cheek. Raj had applied a token of *gulal* on her face. Rashmi didn't know how to respond, Raj also felt uneasy but found courage to say 'Happy Holi'. Rashmi blushed. An uneasy emotion engulfed her. After several decades someone had touched her in this fashion. Her mind went blank. She savoured the moment.

For decades Holi had been a subdued affair in Rashmi's life. She had for long compromised on her destiny. An early marriage, a traumatic miscarriage and a troubled pregnancy had already taken a heavy toll in her life very early. She vividly remembered the time when she had discovered the extra marital affair of her husband. After a protracted divorce she had moved on and lived with her daughter a retired life while she was still in her third decade of life.

Rashmi's daughter found it surprising that this year her mother took more than the usual interest in preparing for the Holi festivities. She found her mother in an unusual happy demeanour.

It was around midnight that Rashmi felt a bout of nausea. The day had been long and strenuous. Visitors had dropped in to say hello. She had also taken the liberty of eating heavy in the evening. Rashmi ignored her nausea and tried to sleep. She reminisced her sojourn to the park with Raj. The thought of Raj with gulal smeared fingers brought a thin smile. Her nausea had receded. She fell asleep.

The second bout of nausea engulfed her sometime around the early morning. She felt sick. Rashmi wanted to yell and call her daughter but her tongue did not move. She made an effort to pick the glass of water from the side table but her hand remained limp. Rashmi realised she had been paralyzed.

Realising that her mother had not come out of her room, Rashmi's daughter decided to check her. Reality dawned as she entered the room. Rashmi lay silent on the bed with her face contorted.

Ambulance was called and Rashmi was carted into the vehicle on the stretcher. The siren of the ambulance made the neighbours curious. The ambulance sped towards the Nazareth hospital. Rashmi was awake but she was unable to move or talk. She heard the shrill siren of the speeding ambulance. The speed of the ambulance slowed; she heard the driver curse the traffic. Someone said that they were passing in front of the St Joseph's college. Rashmi wanted to get up and have a look at the gate. She remembered the day when she first saw Raj.

Raj woke up this morning with thoughts of meeting Rashmi at the St Joseph college gate. He remembered how he had mustered the courage that afternoon when he applied the gulal to Rashmi's face. The sight of a dumbstruck Rashmi with gulal highlighting her flawless complexion was still too fresh in his mind.

Raj reached St Joseph college a few minutes early than his usual time. His eyes kept scanning the road for the glimpse of Rashmi. Minutes passed and it was almost time for the school to give over. Rashmi had not come this afternoon. Raj felt a deep sickening feeling. Suddenly he felt tired.

This afternoon Raj contemplated a thousand different reasons why Rashmi did not come to the college to pick her grandson. In one of the options, he found he was cursing himself of taking the liberty of applying gulal. Was this the reason why Rashmi had opted not to come to the college? Raj felt exhausted. He fell asleep.

The next day, Raj again reached the St Joseph's college a few minutes before his usual time. His eyes continuously looked for the sight of Rashmi. She didn't come. Depression had already crept in Raj's mind. The trees were shedding their leaves in April. The wind had already become laden with dust. Summer was visible. Raj felt he had grown old. His knees today felt heavy.

Rashmi's condition worsened. She found it difficult to focus her thoughts, her mind drifted in states of wakefulness and sleep. She tried to conjure the image of Raj, her mind failed her wish. She slipped in coma. The monitor showing the heart rate and pulse in the ICU became erratic. It took another fifteen minutes for the green florescent line to become straight. The doctor on duty found it routine to pronounce her dead.

In the last few days Raj had found the chore of fetching his grandson from St Joseph's college extremely hard. He felt weak and old. Standing at the gate had become an arduous task. Today as he walked with his grandson up to the car, a vehicle blocked his path. A hearse van was slowly traversing the crowded road. Raj saw the hearse van and said a silent prayer for the unknown person who was being transported for the last time.

6

When destiny beats love

The children had gathered in the courtyard playing cricket oblivious of the sullen atmosphere in the house. The extended family converged in the dingy room where an eighty-five-year-old Salim was awaiting his last few moments of life. His laboured breathing was an indication that the end was near. Salim's daughter Zahida put spoonfuls of sacred *Zam zam* water into the non-receptive mouth reciting the holy Quran.

Salim also had an idea that his end was near. Amidst heavy breathing he beckoned his son Ahmad and daughter Zahida to come near to him. Once close enough, Salim asked them to call for grandchildren Dolly and Yasser. Someone yelled for Dolly and Yasser who were playing cricket in the courtyard. Salim held the hands of Dolly and Yasser and put them one top of the another. Although the children had no idea what this meant, Zahida and Ahmad understood the implications. In this insipid gesture, Salim had created a lifelong bond. Released from the hand of their grandfather, cousins Dolly and Yasser again ran towards the courtyard to resume their unfinished innings of cricket.

Back to Mumbai after the death of her father, Zahida frequently played in her mind the last moments of her father's life. Despite her efforts she could not shrug off her father's last gesture of indicating that she should marry her daughter Dolly with her cousin Yasser. How would this decision play out after two decades when Dolly would be of marriageable age? Would Yasser's upbringing in the small town of Allahabad match with the open atmosphere of Mumbai? Engulfed in these thoughts she would often doze off.

Ahmad had a small business venture in Allahabad. Despite his limited resources, he ensured that Yasser went to the best school in town. He was a bright student and excelled in academics. Yasser had grown enough to realise the implications of his late grandfather's gesture of holding his hand with that of his cousin Dolly. There were few occasions when the extended family would converge in their ancestral house and Yasser could interact with Dolly. Her upbringing in Mumbai made Dolly somewhat misfit in the constrained culture of Allahabad. She still had no idea of her proposed marriage with Yasser.

Dolly was now sixteen years and joined a renowned Mumbai college for higher studies. She was bright in all respects. Her passion for dance and music made her well known among the students even in the first year of college. Having long forgotten the cultural heritage of Allahabad she was now totally in sync with the life in Mumbai.

Yasser's academic journey was limited to the MBA degree from Allahabad University. A lifetime of financial deficit made the decision easy to grab the first employment opportunity that came. Yasser was appointed as an executive in a private company and posted in the eastern UP town of Gorakhpur. Ahmad had a far cousin in Gorakhpur and wanted Yasser to initially live with them before finding a separate house.

Jamshed was a distant cousin of Ahmad and owned a dilapidated house in the old city area of Gorakhpur. He had lost his wife due to encephalitis some five years back. The family now consisted of just a daughter named Rizwana who had barely crossed two decades of life. Jamshed had mixed feelings when he received the call from Ahmad informing that Yasser would live with them for a few weeks. The last time Jamshed had met Ahmad was about fifteen years back in Allahabad when he had paid a condolence visit after the death of his uncle Salim. Jamshed recalled that Yasser was just ten years old when he last saw him.

Rizwana could not recollect having met Yasser before when her father broke the news of someone living with them for a few weeks. The so-called drawing room was rearranged to make way for a sleeping space for Yasser. The initial few days were awkward for the entire family. Yasser would remain confined to his room. Rizwana was always at unease to react in front of an outsider. Her cultural instincts made her extremely cautious of the presence of a male in the house.

In times of loneliness, Yasser sometimes recalled the few memories of Dolly that he had. He could still imagine the moment when grandfather held his and Dolly's hand. The last time he met Dolly was approximately two years back when his aunt Zahida had visited Allahabad for a few days to attend a wedding in the family. Dolly was enticingly beautiful. Yasser had explored ways to interact with Dolly but his efforts could not go beyond the pleasantries. Yasser found it difficult to understand whether Dolly's short attention span was due to lack of interest or preoccupation with ongoing wedding rituals.

Of and on, Yasser had also tried to contact Dolly by email and social media platforms. Her response was always there but somehow Yasser could never sense any romantic affection. He had spoken a few times about Dolly's attitude to his parents but they had always emphasized that grandfather's wish would be respected and that they would be speaking to Zahida to fix the marriage date since Yasser had now got a decent employment.

After a week, the initial hesitation had given way to some intermittent communication between Yasser and Rizwana. She perceived Yasser as an intelligent and well mannered boy. Albeit hesitantly in a few days, Rizwana developed a sense of admiration for Yasser. She had made a mental note of Yasser's likes and dislikes and would try to cook food accordingly. That night when she went to sleep, she found herself humming a film song. She wanted to shrug off the thought but somewhere deep in her heart she felt a soft feeling for Yasser.

It was at the makeshift breakfast table one morning that Yasser broke the news that he had found a room to stay and would most probably shift in a few days. No one spoke. It was a good five minutes later that Rizwana asked Yasser why he wanted to move to another place. Did he find some difficulty here? Yasser didn't react but an unknown evolutionary instinct made him feel better. Today was the first time in almost three weeks that Rizwana had spoken in such a direct manner.

That night when Yasser went to sleep, his mind played back the events of this morning's breakfast. Was Rizwana really concerned about his moving out to another place? He recollected how he felt when a few days back during dinner Rizwana had insistently put a bread in his plate even while he protested that he was full. His mind wandered without any destination. Yasser didn't know when he fell to sleep. *He was playing cricket in the courtyard, Dolly was standing near him. She caught the ball and ran away. He ran towards her but she was running fast..... He wanted to catch her but she ran even faster. She faded away in the air. He yelled Dolly....* Yasser woke up listening to his own voice. He realised he was dreaming and the dream was a disturbing one.

The mornings now had a different flavour in Rizwana's life. She looked forward to making tea and carrying it to Yasser's room. The daily routine of preparing meals was no longer a burden, she started finding ways to cook new dishes. Life had suddenly become more meaningful. That night when she got free time, she gingerly took out the few lipsticks which were a legacy of her mother. Rizwana felt an unknown urge to look beautiful. She applied a lipstick to her lips and saw her image in the mirror. She looked beautiful.

Yasser also perceived the look in Rizwana's eyes. He too felt an urge to talk to her on matters beyond the pleasantries and daily chores. It was Sunday afternoon that Yasser had earmarked for washing his clothes. This afternoon when he made way to the bathroom he found Rizwana washing her own clothes. Before he could trace back his steps, Rizwana apologized and offered to wash his clothes also. His eyes met the sight of Rizwana. There was glint in her eyes. Her hands were full of washing soap. Her unkempt hair accentuated her earthen beauty. Today Yasser realised how pretty Rizwana looked.

It was late evening that Sunday when Yasser received a call from his parents from Allahabad informing that Zahida and Dolly would be visiting Allahabad in a few days and it would be in the fitness of things that the pending marriage gets finalised. Yasser was asked to come to Allahabad for a few days.

With spring in her steps, Rizwana served breakfast to Yasser and her father. It was around second helping that Yasser broke the news that he would be going to Allahabad for a week. In continuation he informed that his parents wanted him to be in Allahabad when his aunt and Dolly come to Allahabad. This could be the occasion when his arranged marriage to Dolly would be finalised.

Rizwana felt giddy. Yasser's information hit her hard. She felt an urge to cry. She remembered the day when her mother had expired. Jamshed felt a lump in the throat. He could sense the feelings of his daughter. For the rest of the breakfast no one spoke. Life resumed in this nondescript Gorakhpur house as usual.

Yasser slept that night with thoughts of Dolly. For a very long time he stared at the photograph of Dolly which he had saved in his mobile phone. Amidst the flow of adrenaline, Yasser went to sleep. *He was playing cricket in the courtyard, Dolly was standing near him. She caught the ball and ran away. He ran towards her but she was running fast..... He wanted to catch her but she ran even faster. She faded away in the air. He yelled Dolly....* Yasser woke up listening to his own voice. He realised he was dreaming and the dream was a disturbing one.

Allahabad was as calm as Yasser had left it two months back. He had brought gifts for his parents. He had also brought an expensive suit for Dolly. It was the next day that Zahida and Dolly were supposed to come. They arrived. Dolly looked all the more beautiful in ripped jeans and cropped top. Two days had passed, there was every kind of conversation but no talk of marriage. It was on the penultimate day of their stay that Ahmad brought up the subject of Yasser's and Dolly's marriage. Zahida didn't speak, however when she did her countenance explained her thoughts before her words did. She informed Ahmad that Dolly was in a live-in relationship with a boy. The din and the commotion of thoughts in Ahmad's mind drowned everything else which Zahida said that afternoon.

After Yasser had left for Allahabad, it took Rizwana two days to come to terms with reality. She had faltered in life by believing that dreams may be true. She rearranged the makeshift drawing room in its earlier format removing the cot which was placed there to accommodate Yasser.

That night Jamshed felt uneasy, his angina pain happened at 2 am but he did not tell Rizwana. The next morning he went to his old friend whose son had recently opened a tailoring shop in the next lane. With tears in his eyes and a lump in his throat, he proposed Rizwana's marriage to his friend's son. In the evening five women visited Rizwana's house with sweets and a few garlands. A ring was placed on Rizwana's finger indicating the confirmation of marriage proposal.

Yasser took the train from Allahabad to Gorakhpur in a hurry. The train which usually takes five hours today seemed undue delayed. He felt an ache in his heart. His mind couldn't distract itself from the sight of Rizwana with soap smeared hands.

The *maulana* was in the last paragraph of his recitation. He didn't need any text to remember his lines. The *maulana* continued informing the groom that his nikah was being solemnised with Rizwana, daughter of Janab Jamshed, with an agreed alimony amount of Rs 25000. The groom answered 'yes'. The motley crowd of *baratis* clapped. In a ceremony lasting barely ten minutes Rizwana's life had taken a new path. Among the onlooking crowd attending the *nikah* ceremony also stood Yasser. Someone pushed a small packet of sugar and dates in his hands, the token of a successful *nikah* ceremony.

7

She said 'take me where you want'

This was indeed an awaited moment for Nilofer. Today she was preparing to go to University as a student of M.A. The thought of being a student of University was far too exciting. She had played out this moment in her mind so many times, now it was going to be a reality. Her mother silently watched with affectionate glee the preparations of her daughter.

All set and done, Nilofer bid goodbye to her mother and took the stairs to step out of the house on the road. Her heart was under the influence of an overdose of adrenaline. Clutching her mobile phone and with a sling bag dangling across her left shoulder, Nilofer stood scanning the road for a rikshaw to proceed to University. It was 9.35 am and she expected to reach the University before the first class which was scheduled for 10 am.

On the same morning, a short distance away from where Nilofer stood waiting for a conveyance, in the nearby side lane, a new beginning was being scripted.

Jamal was getting ready to take out his new e-rikshaw to earn a living. Jamal's countenance betrayed the look of an e-rikshaw driver. Just few months back, Jamal also had dreams of a government job after he finished his MA. Tragedy struck when his father died of COVID. With no income forthcoming, his mother had discussed the option of working as maid but Jamal found it too demeaning. Despite strong opposition from his mother, Jamal decided to leave his ongoing MA course at the University and rented an e-rikshaw on a daily basis.

With tears in her eyes, Jamal's mother patted her son on the cheek and kissed his forehead. Her tears swelled as her thoughts took her to the memory of her late husband. Ahmad loved his only son and wanted him to join a government job. God had other plans. Ahmad could not survive COVID. With his demise, Jamal was left alone to fend the vagaries of life. Today, Jamal was starting a new life as a rikshaw driver.

Gingerly Jamal navigated the narrow lane and found his way to the main road. Dreary eyed, his mother stood at the gate following the rikshaw till the bend at the end of the lane. Jamal had no idea of the intricacies involved in soliciting passengers. Deep in thought of his change in destiny, Jamal heard a call 'rikshaw'. At first, he didn't understand the implication but suddenly realised it was a call that was directed at him. As Jamal's rikshaw came to a halt, Nilofer climbed on the backseat and mumbled 'University'. Jamal did not utter a word and started his rikshaw taking the road towards the University. His mind did register the word University. A few months back he himself was a student of this institution. Life indeed plays cruel pranks, today he was just a rikshaw driver ferrying a passenger to the University.

Nilofer found the atmosphere in the University much to her liking. Her day passed in a flash. She returned home ecstatic and looked forward to the next morning. Jamal found the going tough. As day progressed, he found the long waiting periods between passengers tough to handle. He returned home sullen but concealed his pain when he met his mother at the entrance. The thought of a similar travail the next morning felt heavy. His mind took him to his first passenger, the girl who had boarded his rikshaw to go to University. Despite her face being invisible under the mask, Jamal realised that her eyes exuded an aura of happiness.

Jamal could not sleep. He was still under duress to realise the harsh reality of life. Morning beckoned a new day. His mother prepared food and by 9.30 am Jamal was ready to embark on another day of uncertain fortunes. He took the same road and was still in his blank thoughts till he spotted the girl standing on the side waving in an effort to catch his attention. Jamal recognised she was the same girl who had boarded his rikshaw yesterday to go to University. Jamal paused and the passenger took her seat. She mumbled 'University' and immersed herself on the mobile phone.

Today Jamal got a view of the girl while she took her place in the back seat. Her mask had lost its place and the face was clearly visible. She was beautiful. Jamal focused his thoughts on the traffic ahead winding his way on the crowded street. The turn of events in his life did not provide him the luxury to contemplate on the beauty of the passenger.

Nilofer had no idea that she had boarded the same rikshaw that she took yesterday. She was far too deep in her thoughts to pay heed to the rikshaw or its driver.

Jamal's day was no different from the previous one. There was no joy while he traversed the streets with different passengers all immersed in their own thoughts and preoccupations. There were moments of waiting when he introspected. His thought drifted to the sight of the beautiful girl who had boarded his rikshaw to go to University.

The next morning Jamal, as usual started his rikshaw at 9.30 am As he took the main street, he looked ahead for the sight of the waiting girl. He did locate her, she was standing in front of her house. A strange thought made Jamal happy, he pushed the accelerator to reach her. In a flash another rikshaw went past Jamal and reached the girl. Jamal saw the girl wave to the rikshaw and board it. Jamal reached the spot just 10 seconds later.

Three days had passed and Jamal had picked the tricks of the trade. He had found traffic spots where he could easily find passengers. Despite a good earning, Jamal found it difficult to shirk the disappointment of being a few seconds late before reaching the nameless girl who would go to the University.

Monday was a fresh day. Jamal made an effort to start earlier than usual. He left home at 9.20 am and took the main street. The girl was not in sight. He reached her house and parked his rikshaw in the shade. At 9.30 am she emerged with a sling bag and a phone. Jamal looked towards her. She nodded and boarded the rikshaw. As if on rote she mumbled 'University' and settled on the back seat. Today Nilofer had a chance to see the driver closely. Her mind tried to remember where she had seen this face. A few moments later she realised that she was on the same rikshaw which she had taken to go to University a couple of times. The rikshaw driver looked out of place. Nilofer sensed that there was some weird attribute in the driver which was difficult to explain. Her thoughts drifted and she decided to check her whatsapp.

Jamal sensed a feeling of joy while he drove the rikshaw to the University. An unknown instinct made him connect with this passenger. The girl seemed highly oblivious to his thoughts. She was immersed in her own world.

At last, there was some joy in Jamal's daily routine. He would everyday start in the morning and park his rikshaw in front of Nilofer's house keeping an eye for the time she stepped out. Nilofer also got used to this new turn of events. She would invariably glance towards the rikshaw and without saying anything take the back seat. She again noticed an uncanny look on the driver's face which betrayed the look of a man doing this menial job.

Weeks and months had passed and it was now a routine for Jamal to ferry his passenger to University in the morning. Nilofer found comfort to be able to get the conveyance without waiting. She found the driver a well-mannered boy with gentle behaviour.

Life was indeed flowing smoothly for Nilofer since the time she had got admission in the University. An open academic atmosphere and new friends were all that she could ask for. Everything was fine till something happened which took Nilofer by surprise. One evening some visitors came to her house. By their look the visitors displayed an aura of opulence. The ladies were in heavy makeup and the gents were elegantly dressed. Nilofer's parents instructed her to move to another room. Nilofer realised that the visit had something to do with her marriage proposal.

Nilofer's parents were happy with the new turn of events. They realised that the marriage proposal from such an affluent family was nothing less than a blessing. The prospective boy was projected as the heir to the large business that the family owned. Following the deep-rooted tradition of the family, Nilofer's parents didn't find it important to consult their daughter before taking a decision. The marriage proposal was accepted.

Nilofer's mother broke the news of the impending marriage to her daughter. The sudden turn of events was too big to handle for the girl who had only this year crossed her teen. The joy of completing her studies and then being able to find an independent job vanished in a moment. Nilofer's eyes filled with tears and she cried. Her mother had no idea of the meaning of Nilofer's tears, paradoxically she thought the tears in Nilofer's eyes were an expression of happiness. Life indeed can be deceptive!

The date of the marriage was also fixed without consulting Nilofer. Her mother advised her to stop going to the University and stay at home till the date of marriage. Nilofer did try to convince her otherwise but her mother became adamant. In a 'matter-of-fact' statement she told Nilofer that the prospective groom's family was too wealthy and she didn't need any degrees for a job. That the affluence would keep her happy lifelong.

Nilofer had taken a few books from the University library. She requested her mother to allow her to go to University to deposit the books. She was given permission to go to university but on the condition that she would come back as soon as the work was completed.

Jamal was in a jovial mood. Last night he had a dream which made him happy. He had dreamt that he was driving the rikshaw and the passenger was the beautiful girl going to the University. Somehow the mere thought of the nameless girl evoked a happy feeling.

At 9.20 am Jamal reached the spot where he halted every day to pick the girl. That day he had to wait a bit longer before she appeared. Today she was carrying a lap load of books. Jamal caught a sight of her face. She was not the same as he found her every day. The girl said nothing but Jamal didn't wait for her command. He drove the rikshaw towards the University. Before they reached the University, the girl muttered that she would return in half an hour and that, if possible, he must wait for her at the gate. Jamal waited for her at the gate.

Nilofer returned in 20 min. Jamal realised that she was not carrying the books. Without uttering a word, Nilofer sat on the back seat. Jamal asked where they should proceed. The girl didn't reply. Jamal saw tears flowing down the girl's cheek. Her eyes were red and swollen. Jamal found this situation strange; he too felt a bout of sadness. For no obvious reason he had developed empathy with his nameless passenger.

Jamal repeated the question seeking the destination of the girl while she sat on the back seat. Nilofer had too many thoughts currently on her mind. The last thing she wanted was to return back to the confines of her home. With tears swelling in her eyes, she said to the rikshaw driver 'take me where you want'. Jamal was looking straight at her. He didn't understand the meaning of what the girl said but understood the tone of sadness. He started the rikshaw and took the road towards the girl's house.

Nilofer alighted from the rikshaw and ran towards her gate. Jamal stood watching while the girl walked in urgent strides towards the gate. The girl reached her gate, she paused, before entering the house she looked back towards the rickshaw driver. Her tear-filled gaze met Jamal's sight. Jamal had no idea that this was the last he would ever see of that nameless girl.

The next day morning, with apprehensive and weird thoughts, Jamal waited patiently at the gate for the girl to appear. She did not come out. Jamal felt unhappy but moved on for other destinations.

Several days had passed but Jamal did not get the passenger who used to go to the University. Life again took a new turn and Jamal adjusted in the new normal. Two weeks had passed and Jamal was no longer waiting at the gate of the girl. In free moments he would think of the girl and try to fathom the events of that fateful day when he brought her back from the University. The moment when the girl had looked back at him before entering the gate and met his gaze remained frozen in Jamal's thoughts.

One day while Jamal returned home, he saw the house of the girl illuminated in colourful lights. There was a festive look. Reality dawned on Jamal. What he understood from the illuminating lights did not make him happy. A sense of melancholy engulfed his thoughts.

The wedding was no less than a dream event for Nilofer. She was treated like a princess in her new home. The new found love, the exotic honeymoon and the constant adulation had pampered Nilofer to the extent that she forgot the pains of leaving her study mid-way.

It was a few months past marriage Nilofer realised that sometimes her husband would come home late and be in inebriated state. As time passed these events gained frequency. Nilofer tried to counsel her husband but he would shut her up. On an occasion Nilofer had come across the mobile phone of her husband and to her shock found messages from several girlfriends which were not in good taste.

Nilofer realised that her husband was not enjoying her company any longer. She was reduced to a bystander in the big household basking in the affluence but short on emotional respect. She tried to talk about the situation with her parents but they offered no help, silently everyone wanted her to ignore certain happenings and take life as it is.

Life went from bad to worse for Nilofer. Her husband would openly court other girls. His likes and dislikes were totally against the traditional upbringing of Nilofer. It was a few months short of a year that one day Nilofer walked out of her in-laws place and returned to her parents. Her parents coaxed and cajoled her but her trauma was deep and she resisted all efforts of reconciliation. A couple of months later Nilofer received the divorce papers from her former husband. Nilofer realised that life can also be cruel. With a divorce as her defining attribute she was now expected to spend her life with only a few pleasant memories which remained with her from her brief University sojourn.

Nilofer's father retired from his government job in a few months and the family moved to a new home in the ancestral village far from the city. The change of residence was also dictated by the constant prying of relatives and neighbours seeking details of Nilofer's divorce.

Life brought new fortunes for Jamal. His intelligence and acumen played a part in diversifying his rikshaw trade. Within a year Jamal bought several rikshaw and a few cars to be used as taxi. Now Jamal no longer ferried a rikshaw. He commanded a fleet of rikshaw and cars employing drivers to operate. Good times were here at last in Jamal household.

Jamal's mother felt happy to see her son doing so well. For a few weeks she had been contemplating of finding a life mate for Jamal. She had already sounded a few relatives and friends to suggest prospective proposals. Last week she had visited their ancestral village and came to know about a girl who was perfectly in sync with her traditional thoughts.

It was raining outside; the cool breeze was coming from the open window. Despite the ambient weather, Jamal found it difficult to sleep. On the other bed, his mother too was engulfed in thoughts. Only a mother can understand some situations. She understood that in that motionless pose, Jamal was still awake. She softly called 'Jamal'. Jamal answered 'yes'. She told Jamal that she felt it was time he got married. Without waiting for a reply, she informed that she had seen a girl in their village who would be a perfect mate. At last Jamal found sleep in the wee hours. The sudden turn of events was unexpected. After many months, today he again had the same dream of ferrying a beautiful girl to the University.

Marriage was fixed. The *barat* was a small gathering of close relatives and friends. The red and green tent beckoned the *barat* in the village setting. The *maulana* was brisk in conducting the *nikah*. Jamal was now a married man.

The car marked to bring back the groom and the bride from the village to the city was decked in flowers. Jamal took his seat and was joined by the bride, in heavy embroidered clothes and bright henna. Jamal had witnessed the tearful farewell while his bride left her parents' house. Jamal looked at his wife seated next to him. The veil had slipped and he could see a part of her face and the eyes. There were tears in her eyes. Jamal found a resemblance in those tear-filled eyes. His sight fixed into the gaze of his bride. Jamal remembered the girl with tears in her eyes. Nilofer also remembered the rikshaw driver to whom she had once said 'take me where you want'. Jamal today got the chance to fulfil those words.

8

An ode to a teenage crush

The October morning with a faint chill in the air made a perfect beginning for Zeba as she rubbed her eyes and woke up. As a ritual she stood in front of the mirror and checked herself. She loved her countenance. She realised that of late she felt a strange kind of joy standing before the mirror. It was just a few days back that she had celebrated her 15th birthday. Her mind reminded her that today she had to go to school a bit early keeping a few minutes for a quick visit on way to class teacher's house for picking her homework copy.

A couple of houses across the narrow lane Javed was getting ready to go to University. His mother was also in a hurry arranging breakfast while she got ready to go to school where she taught. She remembered that she had asked a student to collect the homework copy from her house before the school time.

Javed was almost done with his preparations and was about to go downstairs when he heard a knock at the door. His mother was still in the kitchen and yelled to

Javed to open the door. Deep in his own thoughts, with scant enthusiasm, Javed removed the latch and pushed the door open. The person standing on the other side made Javed lose his own thoughts. He was staring at a doe eyed, beautiful girl with a chiseled face, sporting an apprehensive smile. Javed found it difficult to remove his gaze, he was dumb struck for a moment. It took an extended time for Javed to inform his mother that a girl has come from the school. His mother yelled to Javed asking him to give the bundle of copies to the girl. With a lingering smile on her face, Zeba took the bundle of copies and returned. She did not understand why that brief interlude at the door with that unknown boy had made her heart to beat a little faster.

Javed loved cricket more than his studies. This year his performance in the Inter Unit Cricket tournament was appreciated and he had been selected in the University cricket team. While weekdays were spent in the University, on weekends Javed would spend evenings playing with boys in the locality on the small plot of open land which was the only vacant place in the congested locality of closely packed houses.

This afternoon Zeba heard some excitement outside her house and opened the window to see outside. Her window had a clear view of the small vacant plot where she saw some boys playing cricket in fervour. Although she had no inclination towards cricket her eyes caught the sight of the boy whom she had met, albeit fleetingly, while she had gone to her class teacher's house to pick the bundle of copies. The sight of the boy made her continue to watch the game without any understanding of the proceedings. Today she got an extended opportunity to see the boy. He was athletic and good looking. By his mannerisms, Zeba could understand that the boy was good at what he was doing. A strange thought, which was beyond her understanding, engulfed Zeba. She experienced the same exciting feeling which she had felt while she had taken the bundle of copies.

This year Javed did extremely well playing for the University Cricket team. He spent most of his time on the cricket field or in the gym working out to improve his physique. He still found time to play in the locality with friends on weekends. Zeba also kept date with weekend afternoons. Without understanding the game, she found a mysterious pleasure in watching the boy play who, as she understood, was probably the son of her class 10 teacher.

Time passed, Zeba finished school and got into college. For approximately a year she intermittently got a chance to see the boys of the locality play cricket in the vacant plot of land but suddenly one day she saw construction work getting started on that vacant land. It was the last that she saw of the athletically built boy with an attractive gaze who had opened the door on that October morning while she had gone to her class teacher's house to collect copies.

Javed was having a dream run. He got selected in the Uttar Pradesh Ranji Trophy cricket team and now mostly remained travelling following the busy cricketing schedule of the state team. His performance was noticed by the IPL franchises and the same year he was drafted into the Mumbai Indians IPL team. Javed shifted base to Mumbai.

Three seasons passed with Javed playing for the Mumbai Indians. With fame came the money and Javed found himself in the midst of a world full of glitz and glamour. The Mumbai Indians was playing Kolkata Knight Riders in the final of the IPL. It was a high voltage game. With the match tightly poised, Javed went into bat at the fall of second wicket. The bowler started his run and bowled a yorker at 148 km speed, Javed tried to flick but missed. The ball hit his ankle and he fell on the ground. The team doctor came on the field but ruled that Javed had serious injury and cannot continue.

Javed's ankle fracture took a long time to heal. He went into rehabilitation which took another six months. It was almost time for the next season of IPL and Javed was still injured. This season Mumbai Indians didn't select him into their squad. The reality of the life in the fast lane hit Javed hard. A player who just a year back was the toast of the cricket league was now injured and without any financial support.

Zeba was in the final year of college. Nature had bestowed her with a beauty which was ethereal. Despite being a year shy of two decades, Zeba's parents were deluged with marriage proposals. On an occasion when Zeba's mother had discussed with her a possible marriage proposal, Zeba had categorically stated that she wanted to study further and marriage can wait.

Jabir Khan had migrated, as a teenager, to Mumbai from the eastern UP town of Mau about 25 years back.

His was a story straight from a Bollywood thriller. From sleeping on the footpath he had floated businesses which flourished, he now owned palatial houses and property worth several millions. Jabir's underworld links had played a key role in his success.

A far related aunt spoke to Jabir about Zeba and her beauty. Using his relatives in Uttar Pradesh, Jabir sent a marriage proposal to Zeba's parents. Jabir's opulence was far too attractive for Zeba's parents and the consent of the girl became immaterial. The marriage was fixed and very soon solemnized. Zeba went to Mumbai much to her chargrin.

Jabir was a doting husband. He pampered Zeba with all the gifts that money could buy. It was within a year that Zeba was blessed with a baby boy. The initial euphoria for the new bride waned for Jabir. The large age difference between Jabir and Zeba always played in his mind. As time passed Jabir became increasingly possessive of his wife. Zeba felt suffocated in the company of her middle-aged husband and learnt to bide her time with Ismail, her son, who was now almost seven years old.

Watching matches on TV, Ismail had become addicted to cricket. With complete cricketing gear he would pressurize Zeba to take him to school in the evening to play cricket. In a short span of time, Ismail was playing well considering his age. In one of the parent-teacher meetings, the school sports teacher suggested that given his inherent talent, it would be advisable to send Ismail to a cricket academy during the summer vacations.

Jabir Khan too revelled to see Ismail's prowess in cricket. Upon insistence from Zeba, he used his contacts to get Ismail admitted to the cricket academy in Andheri. A driver was specially recruited to daily take Ismail to the cricket academy. Ismail felt more than happy to be coached at the academy.

Once acclimatised into his new surroundings, Ismail became a favourite pupil of the coach at the academy. Ismail too became extremely fond of the coach who, as he learnt, was called Javed Sir by all the students at the academy. Ismail would frequently talk about Javed Sir to his mother and on occasions coaxed her to visit the academy to meet him.

It was Saturday afternoon and Zeba had no pressing engagements at home. It was a long time she had ventured outside their home. Of late Jabir had become unduly possessive and didn't allow Zeba to go alone anywhere. Zeba tutored Ismail to seek permission from dad to allow Zeba to go with him to the academy. Jabir could not refuse his son and he relented to allow Zeba to go to the academy.

The Andheri sports complex was buzzing with activity this Saturday afternoon. At the far end of the stadium were the cricket practice pitches surrounded by nets. A large number of teenage boys were in different stages of getting ready for the practice. Zeba took a seat on the stadium steps far removed from the cricket pitch, from the far distance she could see Ismail getting ready to start his bowling routine. A man in perfect cricketing attire with a red cap was supervising the boys. Zeba could make out that this was Javed Sir, the coach who was addressed in such high esteem by his pupils.

After a couple of hours of intense practice, the cricket trainees dispersed. Ismail ran across the stadium towards his mother. He wanted Zeba to walk down the ground to meet Javed Sir. After some initial hesitation, Zeba walked across the field to the other side where the coach was in the final routine of winding up the session. Zeba could now see Javed Sir closely. Her mind raced to recollect where she had seen this face. Javed was also looking at her, his brain was perplexed, an abstract memory stored in a recess prompted him that the woman standing before him was not unknown. Zeba remembered first, her mind flashed the memory of the boy with the dazed look handing her the copies. Javed's eight billion neurons also brought forth the memory of the doe eyed girl standing on the other side of the gate.

Pleasantries were exchanged. Javed excused himself as he got a call on his mobile. Zeba returned to her waiting car with Ismail. Meeting Javed, her teenage crush, and getting an opportunity to talk to him was so unexpected that she was finding it difficult to understand how to react. Without understanding the meaning, she felt happy.

That evening, Zeba's thoughts frequently went to the chance meeting with Ismail's coach at the academy. The world was in fact a small place. In another room Jabir was in the company of his routine two pegs. The sound system played the Nusrat Fateh Ali's masterpiece 'mere rashke qamar.....'.

A few days passed and Zeba again got a chance to accompany Ismail to the cricket academy. For two hours she watched the proceedings. Although ostensibly she was there to see Ismail play, time and again she found herself a sixteen year old standing in front of the window grill watching the boys play on the small plot of land. Her thoughts were broken by Ismail who came running to her.

In the coming weeks, Zeba found reasons to accompany Ismail. Even without any interaction with Javed, she found the two hours stopover a reason to break free from the suffocating precincts of her home. Watching Javed was always an excuse to go back in time. Jabir did not have interest in her, he was more addicted to his business deals and the late night interaction with friends.

Despite his growing age and an apparent ignorant attitude, Jabir had a sharp acumen. Within a month he realised the change in mood profile of Zeba. His sadistic male instinct prompted him to investigate the reason behind Zeba's new found happiness. His analytical mind shuffled all the possibilities and the changes which might have happened in the last couple of months. He realised Zeba had been going with Ismail without any outward intent. Never before had she ever expressed her interest in cricket. Jabir was certain that the change in Zeba's attitude had something to do with her frequent visits to the cricket academy.

Even after a week, the private detective could not find any clues which could solve the concerns of Jabir based on the brief given to him. He had trailed Zeba twice to the academy and sat at a distance but did not find anything amiss. It was in the second week that the detective chanced upon a hint. The detective told Jabir that the coach Javed belonged to Allahabad and his ancestral house was a couple of houses away from that of Zeba's parents.

Jabir's shrewd mind did not miss the coincidence. He was quick to connect the dots. Jabir understood the implications. He took the decision. A couple of phone calls were made to a few friends.

The two men in track suits alighted from the motorcycle with a kit bag and entered the cricket academy stadium. They walked to the stadium and sat on the last benches under the shade of the tree. Zeba was already sitting at her designated spot and was oblivious of the other two men who sat about 30 yards away from her.

On the other side of stadium, the practice session of the cricket academy had started. Javed Sir was instructing Ismail the nuances of bowling a googly. Once done he handed the ball to Ismail. One of the two men sitting on the other side of stadium opened the kit back and took out a cloth covered stick resembling a hockey. Zeba glanced towards the two men but then again fixed her gaze on Javed. Today in green cap, Javed looked handsome.

The man lifted the hockey shaped structure and pointed it towards the cricket playing group. He took aim, Javed's back was clearly visible in the aim. Ismail was about to bowl having learned the art of googly, he ran and passed Javed before releasing the ball. The ball pitched on the off stump and went towards leg stump.

The batsman thought otherwise and was completely foxed. Ismail jumped in the air and turned around to face Javed Sir.

The man pulled the trigger, even with the silencer in place the rifle emitted a hissing sound. With Diwali round the corner, there was intermittent sound of crackers in the background. The sound of the rifle was lost. The bullet found the left shoulder of Javed just below the neck. A micro second later the bullet came out from the chest caressing the heart in its route. Javed saw the excited look on the face of Ismail but then everything stood still. A gush of blood escaped from his open mouth and he collapsed on the ground.

Commotion followed: The cricket trainees all in their teens were terrified. A few ran towards the coach. Zeba witnessed the fall of Javed and was as bewildered as the trainees. She started running towards Ismail who stood as a statue watching Javed Sir. Zeba caught Ismail and ran towards the exit. She was still shaking when she reached her car.

Zeba was shocked as was Ismail. In the meantime, even before Zeba could reach home, Jabir Khan received a cryptic message, he understood the work has been accomplished. When Zeba reached home she found Jabir in his room. She told Jabir what she had witnessed and also that she had seen the killers from close quarters. Jabir had not foreseen this development. He became unhappy. This was indeed unprofessional on the part of his friends who had handled this liquidation.

Zeba found it difficult to reconcile. The look on the face of Javed while he lay in blood was too fresh in her mind. It was around 10 pm in the night that Zeba called the driver to take her to the graveyard. She was in such a frame of mind that she didn't ask Jabir for the permission. In the graveyard, the formalities of Javed's funeral had just finished. Zeba stood before the grave and prayed. Tears flowed from her eyes. She sprinkled some rose petals on the grave and left.

Jabir was a worried man. He had been contemplating options throughout the evening. Finally he took a decision. Today he exceeded his alcohol content but still he felt tense. Zeba returned and went to her room. She was having a splitting headache. She lay in bed with tears rolling down her cheeks.

In a show of love, Jabir offered a glass of water to Zeba. She found this gesture reassuring. She gulped the water which brought some relief to her taut nerves. Zeba felt her migraine receding. Her head felt light and she felt drowsy. Her mind drifted to a state which was serene.

Jabir realised the drug had worked. He went to the refrigerator and took out the vial of insulin. He took two syringes and filled them with insulin. Zeba was fast asleep under the effect of alprazolam. Jabir pulled her kurta exposing her belly. Under normal circumstances it was proper to wipe the surface with alcohol but this was not normal. He pushed the fine needle and emptied both the syringe in the subcutaneous cavity. Zeba was too sedated to realise what has happened.

Jabir couldn't sleep that night. He watched his comatose wife sitting beside her. There was a time when he was so fond of her. He could now see drops of sweat on Zeba's forehead. Her hands and feet became cold, it took another couple of hours before she stopped breathing.

In the morning news broke out that Zeba had expired while in sleep. It was a consensus that she had suffered a heart attack precipitated by the events related to Javed's murder.

A large number of people had gathered for her funeral. The ambulance carrying the coffin stopped some distance from the graveyard giving a chance to people to participate in the ritual of giving a shoulder to her coffin. Jabir was inconsolable. The grave was already ready. The spot allotted to Zeba's grave was beside a fresh grave which still had some rose petals sprinkled on it. The tombstone standing on the northern side marking the grave had the inscription "JAVED KHAN, 1978 – 2018".

9

Jinxed love and God's wish

Excitement was palpable in the Verma household this Tuesday morning. Sunita woke up early than her usual time; in fact, she had slept only in sporadic intervals during the night. Her mind was continuously preoccupied with the thought of Anuj returning home this afternoon from USA after completing his PhD. For an umpteenth time during the night Sunita had recapitulated in her mind the preparations she had to make for the homecoming of Anuj after three years.

On this Tuesday she left her home early for the visit to the temple to pay obeisance to Lord Hanuman. She had been following this weekly ritual for several decades. In measured steps as she walked the vacant street this morning, her mind took the liberty of going back in time. Sunita's thought catapulted her to the cold December night thirty-two years back when she had taken the seven *pheras* hand in hand with Ashok.

She found herself in perspiration when her mind played the memory of the trauma of not being able to conceive for four long years. She vividly remembered the train visit to Tirupati which Ashok and she took for seeking the blessings of Lord Vishnu in their quest for a child.

Sunita's mind wandered to her most joyful moment of life when Anuj was born a year after their visit to Tirupati. A blissful smile crossed her lips while her thoughts took her through the journey of Anuj's early childhood. He was indeed a bundle of joy. Sunita had almost reached the entrance of the Hanuman temple, she stopped at the small shop selling flowers and as always, she bought some for her obeisance to Lord Hanuman.

Noori woke up as usual this Tuesday morning to the call of *azan* from the nearby mosque. Today she was brisk with her chores, she wanted to reach the bungalow early than usual. Noori was also excited to the homecoming of Anuj. She remembered the birth of Anuj and how as a teenager she would baby sit the newborn with glee. Noori's thought wandered to the trauma of losing her parents while she was a child during the communal riots. She recalled how as a small child she had ran away from her burning house to safety escaping the rampaging violence and how she had found a home which provided her shelter.

It has been forty years since Noori had lived in the outhouse of the bungalow owned by Ashok Verma. She had become a member of the household ever since. The Verma family reposed as much faith in Noori as they would do to a close family member. Young Anuj always found solace in the arms of Noori when his tantrums, as a child, would be ignored by parents. Noori remembered how Ashok and Sunita had requested the local mosque cleric to teach young Noori the Quran and the tenets of Islam. Noori's thought took her to the moment when the Verma family had played the role of a perfect host to the *baraat* which heralded her *nikah* to Abdul.

As Noori finished her morning prayer this Tuesday morning she prayed for the safe flight of Anuj. Her gaze moved to the nearby cot where Zoya, her daughter, was in the process of waking. Noori reminded Zoya to wake up and offer the morning prayer before it became late.

By late afternoon the Verma household wore a festive look. Ashok and Sunita were almost ready to go to the airport to receive Anuj. Noori had made an assortment of delicacies which in her opinion were Anuj's favourites. Zoya had pitched in with cleaning and putting things in order. As a mark of importance for the occasion, both Noori and Zoya had put on their best clothes. With youth on her side, the twenty-two-year-old Zoya looked vivaciously pretty.

Three years in the cold US climate had made Anuj almost two shades fair. He had also gained some weight. As he came out of the airport terminal, Anuj scanned the waiting crowd for his parents. Sunita could not control the involuntary tears which swelled in her eyes when her gaze met that of Anuj. In that red jacket with black Rayban glasses, to her mother's eyes Anuj resembled a Greek god. With a lump in his throat and a beaming smile, Ashok hugged Anuj.

The homecoming was complete. Anuj looked for things and felt happy when he realised that very little has changed while he was away from home. In Noori aunty he still found the same soft shoulder where he could get his tantrums resolved. Anuj found the most remarkable change in Zoya. Three years back when he had left for US, Zoya was a teenager and looked a chirpy girl. In the last three years, Anuj realised that Zoya had transformed. She was indeed pretty.

Zoya's upbringing had inculcated in her the habit to hide her feelings in public. She found it natural to be comfortable always in the background. This afternoon, while everyone interacted with Anuj, she was contended to witness the festivities from the kitchen door. Despite her unwillingness to come to the fore, she could not resist the flight of her mind which instigated a primordial basic instinct. She did find Anuj handsome. It was just three years back when she would gleefully talk to Anuj who was just five years older to her. She remembered the days when as a teenager Anuj would play cricket with friends and she would be a part of one of the teams. Today she experienced an unknown hesitation in initiating a conversation with Anuj.

The following days after Anuj's arrival were stamped with joy for the Verma family. The mood in the family was picture perfect. Anuj had melted into his old routine without any difficulty. Noori aunty tended to his personal requests. Even Zoya had started conversing with him. He found it interesting to share the college life of US with Zoya. He found a perfume bottle in his luggage which he wanted to give to Zoya. An unknown instinct made him look for a private setting to gift it to Zoya. It was a few weeks after his return that during dinner Sunita initiated the conversation of his possible marriage. With no effort to conceal the conversation, Sunita and Ashok discussed the attributes of Poonam, the daughter of their long time friend Vivek who owned several hotels in the city. Anuj offered no response.

After repeated requests and cajoling from Sunita and Ashok, Anuj met Poonam as part of a dinner date. Anuj found Poonam to be a simple girl with no bearing of a rich legacy. In that maroon top, Poonam looked stunning. Even before they had ordered dessert, Anuj was already looking forward to his next meeting with Poonam.

Given the approval of parents, finding opportunities for rendezvous with Poonam was not a problem for Anuj. He found that Poonam had completed her graduation from a prestigious college and was interested in pursuing a career in fashion industry. She was soft spoken and a good listener. Anuj felt nice to learn that Poonam was a vegetarian.

Poonam found Anuj handsome. Some strange evolutionary instinct made her happy in his company. She realised she felt secure when Anuj was around. And therefore when, exactly six weeks later when they had first met, Anuj proposed to her while they walked hand in hand in that soft drizzle of July, Poonam did not hesitate to put her hands around his neck and whisper a soft yes!

Amid festivities the two families met over dinner to chalk out the programme of the marriage. The priests in attendance on the occasion proposed the best date for the marriage. On the insistence of Sunita and Ashok it was decided that the reception menu would be totally vegetarian. Sunita recalled that she had vowed to become a strict vegetarian, as per religious commandments, ever since she had gone to Tirupati to seek blessings of Lord Vishnu exactly twenty-eight years before.

The festivities of the engagement ceremony extended late until midnight. Poonam was the cynosure of the ceremony. In pink ensemble complete with tiara she looked ethereal. The soft tune of Jagjit Singh ghazal filled the air. The moment had arrived for Anuj to place the ring on her finger. As she watched Anuj walk towards her, her eyes drooped. She felt giddy, a bout of nausea engulfed her. She lost balance. Commotion ensued but soon she regained her composure. The ring finally found its place on the delicate third finger of the left hand.

Anuj realised that good times never pause, days seem to pass by in a hurry. Every moment spent with Poonam was worth a lifetime. He would always learn new things about Poonam which made him yearn for more time to spend in her company. He had become obsessed.

Poonam again felt giddy. Her episodes of transient passing out had returned in the last few days. She felt tired. Was it the effect of her emotional euphoria which was making her tired? She wondered. Just as her mind had started exploring difficult health options, her phone rang. Anuj was on the line. His voice made her lift herself. She remembered she was being late for the date.

The date of their wedding was fast approaching. Three days separated Anuj and Poonam to be legally bound into the lifelong association. Anuj suggested that they would observe a hiatus for three days. This would again be more romantic than be constantly in touch. Thus, it was mutually decided that now they would see each other only after marriage.

It was during night while she was changing clothes that Poonam saw some red patches on her skin. Although she had became used to her constant fatigue, this new observation made her worried. She made a mental note to visit the doctor the next morning.

Lest no one became unduly concerned, Poonam made her visit to the doctor as discreet as possible. The doctor took down her history and made careful observations. Before making any diagnosis, the doctor prescribed some pathological tests. Poonam went directly to the pathology and gave her samples.

A night separated the marriage date. The Verma household was bathed in joy. The extended family had converged to take part in the celebrations. The *dholak* found no respite till the wee hours. Anuj wanted to talk to Poonam but the joy of observing the self-imposed restriction was too romantic to be breached. Despite having spent a considerable time with Poonam, Anuj day dreamed a thousand options he would indulge after marriage in the company of his beloved Poonam.

Poonam again had to find a benign alibi to visit the doctor for the diagnosis and pathology report. On an obscure reason she did find an excuse to be away from the celebrations for a brief moment. After a waiting of fifteen minutes she was ushered in doctor's chamber. The look on the face of the doctor was not enthusiastic. In clinical terms, he explained to Poonam that the initial findings and the symptoms probably point out to the first stage of leukemia or blood cancer.

Poonam could find just enough strength to return home. Her mind was in a spin. The news had given her a second wind. For a short time she forgot her fatigue. On an impulse she picked up the phone and wanted to talk to Anuj but then visualised his beaming countenance and decided against breaking this news to him. She did not want to spoil his joy. She lost her count of the options she explored to cope with the present crisis.

It was dinner time and Poonam had not joined her friends and parents at the table. Someone yelled to Poonam to come down for dinner. Her friends joked that she must be busy talking with Anuj. It was around eleven at night that someone suggested to check with Poonam. The door was bolted from inside. She was also not picking the phone. Enthusiasm had transformed into anxiety. The door was finally broken. Poonam lay on the bed her hand revealing the deep cut on the wrist. A pool of blood had soaked her hair and the bedsheet.

News travelled fast to the Verma family. The *dholak* became silent. Anuj thought he was dreaming. He picked the phone and frantically called Poonam. His Poonam always picked his phone on the first ring, today the phone defied the romance that had became synonymous with these lovebirds for the last couple of months. Anuj realised the reality of Poonam's death. He could not muster the courage of attending her last rites.

Six months had passed since Poonam's death but Anuj could not come out of his mourning state of mind. For days he would remain confined to his room. The Verma household remained perpetually gloomy. Sunita and Ashok explored the possibility of visiting Tirupati to seek divine help for bringing good times to the family again. Noori was entrusted the responsibility of the household while Sunita and Ashok went to Tirupati Balajee.

Noori took extra care of Anuj in Sunita's absence. She found ways to cajole Anuj into eating his favourite dishes. While Anuj sat on the dining table, Noori would delve into his childhood anecdotes in her effort to uplift his spirits. This afternoon while Noori served lunch to Anuj, the routine atmosphere was suddenly punctuated by the entry of a jubilant Zoya carrying a small box of sweets. Oblivious of the presence of Anuj, Zoya ecstatically announced that she had passed her M.A. examination in first division. The lively announcement also made Anuj take notice of the intruder. Anuj looked towards Zoya, her ebullience was infectious. His eyes caught the sight of Zoya's gaze. In that moment of exuberance, Zoya looked beautiful. Anuj realised he had to make an extra effort to move his transfixed eyes away from Zoya.

About the same time, almost a thousand kilometres away at Sri Venkateswara Swamy Vaari Temple, Sunita and Ashok were deep in prayers seeking Lord Vishnu's divine blessings for happiness to return in Anuj's life.

That night, as Anuj lay in bed, his mind recollected the ecstatic moment of a beautiful Zoya asking him to share sweets in celebration of her academic achievement. He realised that he had not interacted with Zoya for several months. Zoya's youthful exuberance had an intensity which was indeed highly attractive.

The next morning Anuj woke up early. With no predetermined thought, he walked out of the bungalow towards the outhouses where Noori and Zoya lived. The sun was still below the horizon but there was enough light for Anuj to see the inside of the room. The door was slightly open and Anuj peeped inside. The prayer mat was neatly laid out, Zoya was praying. In that moment when Zoya stood before her Almighty with her head covered with a scarf, Anuj saw the portrait of bliss. Anuj stood in trance, he was enchanted. He waited for Zoya to complete her prayer.

Zoya opened her eyes after the prayer to find Anuj standing at the door. A thousand thoughts flashed in her mind however none could decipher correctly what was going on in Anuj's mind. She looked towards Anuj with a perplexed innocent smile. As if on cue, Anuj took a step inside the room. He could now see Zoya closely. The unblemished face looked enticingly beautiful. Anuj hesitantly came closer; three words escaped his lips. Zoya heard the three words which till now she had only heard in bollywood films. She didn't know how to answer; she covered her face in both her hands and ran inside.

Sunita and Ashok returned with peace of mind. They had prayed to the Lord to once again bring happiness in Anuj's life. To their great relief, the parents found Anuj in a cheerful mood. The family had dinner together.

Sunita heard something moving. She realised it was beyond midnight. She put the lamp on. Anuj was standing at the bedside. The sudden movement also made Ashok to wake. Both the parents looked dazed. Their looks beckoned Anuj to explain his presence in their bedroom such late at night. Anuj searched for words, when he found his voice, he could only say that he wanted to marry Zoya.

For a moment Sunita didn't acknowledge what she had just heard. Ashok felt a bout of headache. No one spoke for a couple of minutes. Anuj meantime had left the room. Sunita and Ashok remained awake for rest of the night. There was very little to discuss though.

No one initiated any conversation during the breakfast. Noori did not come to the bungalow this morning. Perhaps she was also contemplating the effects of what Anuj had told Zoya.

The marriage was a private affair. In exquisite Sherwani Anuj again visited the outhouse but this time a few friends accompanied him. In bright red traditional clothes Zoya looked a princess. The *nikah* was solemnised by the local cleric. The same evening the Verma bungalow wore a festive look. A *mandap* was built within the lobby.

Under the watchful eyes of the head priest, with Sunita and Ashok in attendance, Zoya walked hand-in-hand around the fire taking the traditional wedding vows.

Sunita had problem in her knees, she had started using a wheelchair. On this Tuesday morning, while Zoya pushed her wheelchair on the street towards the Hanuman temple, Sunita felt nice. She found the same florist at the entrance of the temple.

10

Who killed Roshni?

The perspiration on the forehead was palpable. For an umpteenth time, he changed his sleeping position that night but found it difficult to sleep. The events of the previous evening were too heavy on his mind. The man who had visited him that previous evening had not divulged much but had given an indication that he was interested in finding about the accident. It's been almost a month since that terrible accident when his truck had rammed into a Maruti 800 on the highway. For a few weeks, after the accident, he was frightened that his truck would be identified and he would be arrested but nothing had happened. The sudden turn of events was unexpected. This was the reason why he was still awake tonight while the wall clock indicated it was 3 am. It was around 3.30 am that he finally dozed off.

Manoj and his wife had been married for many years but the joy of a child had eluded their married life. The initial euphoria of marriage had waned and had given way to a sense of desperation as far as their married life was concerned. Manoj had consulted several doctors but Reena could not conceive. It was in the seventh year of their marriage, after they had returned from Khwaja's Dargah in Ajmer, that Reena broke the news to Manoj that she was expecting. Eight months later their bundle of joy Roshni was born.

Roshni was the toast of the family, all the joy revolved around her. On her part, Roshni displayed qualities which made Manoj and Reena proud. She was ebullient and lively excelling in studies and sports. Roshni had an interest in biology and wanted to become a doctor. Manoj and Reena doted on her child and always made efforts to give her the best environment. Time flew fast for the Sharma family while Roshni became a teenager.

Roshni was preparing for the NEET examination which was scheduled on the coming Saturday. The examination center was a bit far and Manoj took leave from the office to drop Roshni to the examination center. This Saturday while Roshni prepared for the examination, her parents prayed in the nearby temple. It was almost time and Manoj started his old Maruti 800. Manoj prided his Maruti 800 and had always found ways to change the topic when friends chided him for purchasing another car. This was the same car which was a companion to his fond memories of long drives during the initial years of marriage.

The Saturday morning was quiet in terms of traffic on the highway. The four lane highway was ommissioned just a year back and had cut down travelling time. Manoj, now in the sixth decade of his life, as a habit never exceeded the speed of 60 km per hour. There was a time when he would be offended by overtaking vehicles but age has had a gradual mellowing effect. He had silently adopted the maxim 'better late than never'.

While Manoj navigated the highway keeping his car in the left lane, Roshni sat on the passenger seat delving deep into the Chemistry book. At times Manoj's sight drifted towards her daughter but he didn't want to disturb her. In those fleeting glimpses Manoj realised his mind was looking at a future young doctor with a stethoscope around her neck.

Manoj's sight caught the sudden movement in the rear view. In that instant he saw a truck inching towards his car from behind. The truck was in high speed. Manoj swerved his car to the left almost touching the kerb. The truck was now inches away, it veered towards right but brushed the car from behind. The car lost balance and hit the highway fence. Manoj saw the left door open on impact plunging Roshni out of the car. This was the last Manoj remembered.

Manoj was discharged from the hospital two days later after treatment for concussion and minor bruises but he was informed that the doctors could not save Roshni. Manoj wept. For days he was inconsolable as was Reena. Life became cruel. The realisation that they would now have to complete their remaining lifespans with only memories of Roshni was too harsh for Manoj and Reena.

The Police lodged an FIR and also recorded Manoj's statement but nothing happened. There were no other witnesses to this accident. Roshni's death had no political value and thus became just a file in Police records. For few days the Police was receptive to Manoj's queries but after a week even the phone calls were seldom received and rarely answered.

Manoj would regularly go to the highway and sit on the pavement where the accident had happened, gazing into oblivion. Countless times he found his mind wavering to the memory of Roshni sitting on the passenger seat while he drove the car on the highway. The highway fence still had some scars of the car hitting it but other than this the highway was unchanged. There was a regular stream of vehicles speeding on the four-lane tarmac.

It was after ten days that Manoj decided to find ways to piece together the events of that fateful day. His science background made him think analytically. He started counting the number of trucks passing through that stretch of highway during 9 am and 10 am. The last toll plaza was just three kilometer behind and the next toll plaza was fifty five kilometers from this place. Manoj observed that eighty-three trucks passed through on this Thursday. Manoj repeated this exercise for the next few days and found that on an average approximately 80 to 90 trucks passed the highway during the morning hours between 9 am and 10 am.

Back home Manoj tried hard to find some clues from his observations but he could find no coherence. It was way past midnight while Reena slept, that Manoj got an idea. He realised that all the trucks passing through the highway were moving at more or less similar speeds. His analytical thinking prompted him to realise that the first reaction of a driver after hitting a vehicle would be to escape from the scene of accident. This would inherently involve driving at a faster speed. Manoj found this explanation of his mind quite logical. Contemplating his inference, Manoj went to sleep.

In the morning Manoj again revived his thoughts. As much as he thought, his hypothesis became clearer. He realised he had stumbled upon a logical algorithm to trace the truck driver who had hit his car on that fateful Saturday.

Working on his hypothesis, Manoj's next stop was the preceding toll plaza on the highway. He found that the persons manning the toll plaza were far from being classified as polite. It was even difficult to strike a conversation. After weighing options, Manoj decided to use the tried and tested method of getting things moving fast. He took out a Rs 500 bill from his purse and pushed that into the hand of the person on duty at the booth. In a few minutes Manoj was able to get the information which he wanted. The toll plaza attendant handed him the printout of the registration numbers of heavy vehicles which passed through the toll gate on the date which Manoj had indicated.

Armed with the information which he got from the first toll plaza, Manoj went to the next toll plaza on the highway which was approximately 58 kilometer away. The attitude of the people at the toll plaza was no different, no one was willing to talk to Manoj. Here again the tried and tested power of the money came in handy. Within fifteen minutes Manoj got the printed list of vehicle numbers which had passed through this toll gate between 10 and 11 am on the date which Manoj indicated.

That night Manoj went about methodically in analyzing the two lists which he had got from the second toll plaza. Manoj recalled that it was twenty-three minutes past ten when the accident had happened. A truck passing through the accident spot would have to travel fifty-five kilometers to reach the next toll gate. He marked the numbers of all the trucks which had passed through the first toll between 10 am and 10.30 am. On that Saturday, Manoj observed, a total of thirty-five heavy vehicles had passed through the toll within this time period. He then checked the arrival of these thirty-five vehicles at the next toll gate.

Weaving through the data Manoj observed that on an average the heavy vehicles had taken fifty two/fifty three minutes for traversing the distance of fifty eight kilometers between the first and second toll booths. His observation was punctuated by some figures which did not match the general trend. Manoj observed that four heavy vehicles passing through first toll gate at around 10.10 am and 10.20 am had reached the second toll gate taking significantly less time than the average. The average time taken by these four vehicles was forty four/ forty five minutes. Manoj jotted down the registration numbers of these four vehicles. His mind was already engrossed in permutations and combinations.

The Regional Transport Office was housed in a nondescript building within narrow streets flanked by shanties housing the makeshift offices of touts. Manoj gingerly entered the office and looked for the directions to the Assistant Regional Transport Officer. A black and white wooden board displayed the name Atul Hajela, ARTO. Manoj's mind went into overdrive, the name Atul Hajela evoked a sense of déjà vu. It was in school some four decades back that he had a friend who had the same name. As Manoj entered the office, his gaze met that of the officer sitting on the other side of the table. Atul recognised him instantaneously.

It took another hour while the office of the RTO gave Manoj the address and names of the owners of the four vehicles which found mention in his list based on the time taken to complete the distance between the two toll booths. A phone call from Atul Hajela to the owners resulted in a second list with names, phone numbers and address of drivers of those vehicles.

Manoj felt satisfied with the progress he had made in the last two days. The drivers of the vehicles lived in different cities. Two drivers lived in Allahabad, one in Kanpur and one in Azamgarh. Manoj realised that the next step was going to be tricky. He decided to start from Allahabad.

Jagram sweet shop was an easy location to find. The shop situated on the busy crossing was already brimming with activity when Manoj entered to look for directions to the house number 245 Mumfordganj, beside the carpentry school. The owner, already indulging in a mouthful of gutka, didn't speak but pointed to the lane beside the shop. Manoj reached the house which was the last one in the narrow lane. There was no bell so he shook the chain dangling from the door knob so as to make a noise. It was after two such episodes that a small girl answered in an enquiring tone.

Suresh was in his early forties, he ushered Manoj into a makeshift tin roofed room which had two rickety chairs and a cot. From the look, Manoj could understand that his host seldom hosted any unknown visitors. Suresh had no idea why an unknown person had sought his attention by paying a visit. Manoj did not take long to come to the point. He discreetly asked Suresh whether he remembered driving his truck on NH 19 about fifteen days back. Suresh smiled fleetingly, he told Manoj that he has been driving his truck almost every day and frequently takes NH 19. The look on Suresh's face was genuine. Manoj could not sense any attempt to conceal any event.

The conversation meandered further and Manoj could not hide his real reason of visit. He confided to Suresh that he was trying to find the truck which rammed his car on that fateful Saturday morning resulting in the death of his daughter. The look on Suresh's face changed, he became animated. He told Manoj that he remembers the sad event which he witnessed while he was passing NH 19. He told that after passing a few kilometers from the toll booth, he had seen in the far distance a truck suddenly changing lanes and then an accident with a white small car. He told Manoj that he accelerated his vehicle to catch the truck which had caused the accident but the other truck was driving at high speed. He continued to chase the speeding truck for the next forty minutes but could not overtake. It was on the next toll booth that he lost sight of the truck in front. Suresh confided that he felt sorry for the car which met with the accident.

The old city of Allahabad was bustling with activity with petty traders while Manoj snaked his way through the dingy lanes and bylanes. It took Manoj a good fifteen minutes to reach the house of Jameel. He met Jameel in front of his house. Jameel looked apprehensive. Manoj framed the same questions to Jameel as he had put before Suresh. Jameel did remember driving through NH 19 on that Saturday morning. He told Manoj that, in fact, after that date he became ill and had not taken out his truck. Jameel told Manoj that on that day he was not feeling well and had given the driving to his nephew who worked as a cleaner in the truck. Jameel told Manoj that he specially remembers that day because despite his repeated warnings, his nephew had speeded the truck overtaking all other vehicles. He remained ignorant of any accident on the way while he went through the distance between the two toll booths.

The area of Gwaltoli just adjacent to the Civil Lines in Kanpur housed a slum which had developed on the embankment parallel to the defunct Lal Imli railway line. Manoj found Deepak alone in his dingy room which had barely enough space for a cot. Deepak was in his late fifties but displayed a countenance much beyond his age. As Manoj stood in front of the door the stench of smoke from cheap cigarette reached his nose, Deepak rose from the cot and moved out making a gesture to talk to Manoj in the lane which provided the only free space. Manoj was ready with his questions. Deepak listened to Manoj with an abstract look. He said that he had no specific memory of driving his truck at a fast speed between the two toll booths. He had also not seen any accident that day on the highway.

The village of Walidpur in Azamgarh was a quiet hamlet on the banks of the river Tons. The makeshift bazaar was in full bloom when Manoj reached the tea stall where Sabir was sitting with a few friends. Sabir was taken by surprise when Manoj introduced himself as an insurance agent. Sabir had no idea why any stranger would be interested in talking to him. He was a man of meager means driving a truck for earning a living. When Manoj opened further enquiring about his journey through the NH 19 on that fateful Saturday, Sabir heaved a sigh. Sabir told Manoj that while he was passing through the first toll booth he had received a phone call from his wife who was full time pregnant. She had informed him that she had started labour and needed to go to hospital. Sabir had driven as fast as possible to reach his place. With a faint smile Sabir said that he had been blessed with a baby boy. Manoj left.

Back home, Manoj pieced together the information he had gathered in the last few days. At least one driver had confided to have seen the accident, however his observations provided no clue to the identity of the driver who drove that truck which hit the car. It was reasonable to assume that Jameel's nephew, who was not a professional driver, may have hit his car. Deepak could be an equal suspect, he looked to be harboring a few addictions and portrayed a dicey character. Even Sabir may be a suspect who could be using his wife as an alibi. Manoj was lost in thought, he needed to understand the psychology of a criminal to get to the culprit.

In recent times, the Wheeler Book Shop in Civil Lines, Allahabad had significantly lost its sheen. Once a rendezvous of intellectuals, the book shop now had but a few visitors. As Manoj entered the shop on that Monday morning, he felt a tryst with knowledge. The soft voice of Mehdi Hasan ghazal playing somewhere added to the ambience. After leafing through countless books, Manoj hit upon the book he was looking for, he purchased Investigative Psychology by David Canter and walked out of the book shop.

The next few days Manoj devoted his time to read the book he had bought from Wheeler Book shop. The book provided him with the understanding of the thought process of a criminal. Manoj came up with a plan.

He opened the gallery of his mobile phone and scrolled through the photographs of the accident which he had obtained from the police records. There were gruesome pictures of Roshni in blood with the overturned car. With tears in his eyes and a lump in his throat, Manoj selected two pictures of the accident site and attached them through WhatsApp to four mobile numbers.

Suresh was getting ready to take out his truck for another arduous day in which he would be travelling six hundred kilometers passing through NH 19. His daughter had prepared a frugal breakfast. He glanced at his mobile phone. There was a whatsapp message from an unknown number. Suresh saw the message, there were two photographs of an accident in the message. His mind raced to the memory of the gory accident he had witnessed approximately one month back while travelling through NH 19. The sight of the teenage girl lying in blood made him feel sick. He remembered how he had chased the speeding truck for about fifty kilometers but had lost sight at the next toll booth. He had no idea why this message was sent to him. He decided to ignore it but then, at second thought, decided to send a 'weeping' emoji as a reply. The day had not started on a good note.

Jameel was sitting in the waiting area of a doctor's clinic for his turn when he got a notification. He glanced at the whatsapp message from an unknown number. He could not make out any sense of the two photographs except that the sight of the blood-stained girl was difficult to look at. At that moment the reception called out his name and Jameel walked into the doctor's chamber.

This evening Deepak had invited a few friends at his shanty. It was a fun filled evening with country liquor and non-vegetarian food on offer. Deepak had overeaten and then slept under the influence of alcohol. Deepak saw the whatsapp message the next day at 10 am. At the first sight his groggy eyes could not make out the details but a few moments later he realised the gravity of the message. Someone had sent to him the photographs of the accident which happened approximately a month back when he was driving his truck on NH 19.

Deepak felt jittery. He knew someone was on his trail and had identified him. He remembered the visit of that unknown person some two weeks back who was enquiring about the accident. Fear engulfed Deepak, he knew he had little time. He fished out some money from the overhead box and bolted his shack. He took the bus and reached his village.

Sabir too got the message but had no idea why he had received this message. He deleted the message without any second thought.

The weeping emoji from Suresh was enough to convince Manoj that Suresh was telling the truth. Now only three suspects needed to be investigated. Manoj decided to visit Deepak, Jameel and Sabir.

Manoj went to Azamgarh and met Sabir in the village bazaar. Sabir was buying vegetables. He recognised Manoj and enquired about his wellbeing inviting him to come to his house for a cup of tea. Manoj moved on. He took the train to Allahabad. He reached Jameel's house in the congested Shahganj area. Jameel's teenage son informed that Jameel had gone to a doctor. Jameel came back in an hour, he looked ill. After a brief conversation Manoj could sense that Jameel was not perturbed at seeing him again. Manoj moved on. He took the evening train to Kanpur.

Manoj reached Deepak's room beside the railway track in the morning. The narrow lane was bustling with activity. A sweetmeat shop selling breakfast items was crowded with customers. Manoj reached the end of the lane where he had met Deepak. The room was locked. He asked a few passersby about Deepak. Somebody told him that Deepak had not come home for the last three or four days. No one had any idea about his whereabouts.

Two days later, with all the investigative evidence, Manoj visited the office of Senior Superintendent of Police. Fortunately, the officer was an alumnus of Allahabad University and turned out to be a hostel mate of Manoj's elder brother in the Muir hostel. Within days the police arrested Deepak. A forensic examination of his truck revealed traces of paint of the Maruti 800 car on the front. The forensic report also observed evidence of dents on the left side of the front bumper.

Deepak confessed to have been drunk while he drove his truck on the NH 19 on that Saturday morning. The sessions judge took cognizance of the crime and sentenced Deepak under IPC section 80.